DIVING IN WITH ALIOTH

MEGHAN MONARCH

MEGHAN MONARCH LLC

DEDICATION

For those of you wanting nothing more than to be your true, authentic self...
BE it.

A NOTE TO THE READER

Dear Reader,

Thank you for deciding to give *Diving in With Alioth* a chance! I hope you love reading it as much as I loved writing it. My goal with this book is to make you blush, smile, and laugh.

This story is full of low-stakes, high-steam, fun, and comedy. In my opinion—although biased—it's a fun time.

That being said, if you are interested in knowing any possible triggers or important reading details, you can find them in the next paragraph, as well as on my website, where you can also find categories and other scaled ratings for each of my works. Not everyone likes surprises, and protecting yourself as a reader and a human being is important. If you'd rather not read the list, I suggest flipping the page to skip that.

And, if as a reader, you notice a trigger warning I may have missed—because I am far from perfect—please let me know so I can add it to the list on my website.

Diving in With Alioth includes: profanity, one brief mention of the 2020 COVID outbreak, the FMC working toward overcoming her fear of water and swimming (which includes swimming lessons given by our alien MMC), a moment where our FMC is taken under the water without warning, graphic sex, casual sex, sex in a car, a pool, and a hair salon, sex between a human and an alien, alien transformation from humanoid to true alien form, and mentions of an alien invasion of the friendly kind.

Please read with care and enjoy your journey.

XOXO,

Meghan

ONE MORE THING

Dear Reader,

I think it's important to note something I've purposefully done with this series in order to, hopefully, make everyone understand my intentions behind the decision, and know that I have truly dedicated my time and energy to ensure I've followed the proper steps to do this accurately and respectfully, seeing as there is always a risk of this book making its way into someone's hands who maybe has never heard of me before, and therefore, might not know where I stand.

In the Mate-Cute Series, you will notice that I do not go into super specific physical details regarding any characters outside of our alien main characters. That is for a specific reason—so that readers may have an easier time picturing themselves as our lead.

That being said, I know that brings about a risk of some of you questioning things about those characters that aren't exactly described in detail, especially regarding you as an individual, and how their life, choices, and story relate to you. And I want to make sure I touch on that.

All of the characters you meet in this series are easily seen in my mind. I have pictured all of them before writing them on paper, even if you see them differently from me. And I want you to know that any characters written in this series that differ from me in any way—be it race, gender identity, religion, mental health struggle, etc.—I have taken the time to search and work with sensitivity readers on to ensure I treat every character and situation with the thoughtfulness and care they all deserve.

If you ever have any questions about any of this, never hesitate to reach out.

XOXO,

Meghan

PRONUNCIATION GUIDE

CHARACTERS

- **Alioth**: Uh-lie-uth (Our MMC's name)

- **Kiran**: Keer-in (Another alien included in the story)

OTHER DYV'I INFORMATION

- **Spa'Wa:** Spah-wah (The name of Alioth's restorative bath spa)

- **Cēd**: Seed (The name of Kiran's greenhouse)

- **Agri'vi**: Uh-gree-vee (The name of a Dyv'i restaurant the couple visits)

ALIEN BACKGROUND INFORMATION

- **Dyv'i**: Dye-vee (The alien species that invaded Earth in 2020)

- **Dyv'iëdus**: Dye-vee-eh-duhs (The alien planet the Dyv'i traveled from)

- **Wa'gōah**: Wah-go-uh (Alioth's Dyv'i subspecies)

- **Cēd'oh**: See-doh (Kiran's Dyv'i subspecies)

PROLOGUE

When aliens touched down on Earth five years ago, there were various reactions from people all over the planet. Some screamed and hid like in the movies, others were curious and open to learning more, while the rest—mostly millennials—weren't fazed one bit and kept going to work like normal fucking human beings.

What we didn't know then that we do now is that these aliens are shapeshifters. Known as the Dyv'i, they walk around in human-like forms until they encounter their mates—and when they find them and fall in love, their mate is the only one who will ever see them in their true form. Sure, some of them fall in love with each other, but they most often fall in love with humans, which is why so many of them wound up traveling here and choosing to stay.

Welcome to Earth in the year 2025, where instead of the coronavirus outbreak five years back, there was an alien invasion of the friendly kind.

In this series, you'll encounter novellas filled with alien romance, out-of-this-world spice, and lots of surprises.

Will your fated mate be from another planet?

CHAPTER ONE

WREN

"New decade, new Wren, Thea!" I shout from the driver's seat of my car as I park along the downtown street.

She laughs through the speaker. "I get that, but are you sure you *really* want to do something like this on the first day of your thirtieth year? You're afraid of water."

I huff. "I'm not going swimming, just relaxing in a Dyv'i salt bath. Apparently, they make you float and cleanse your body of aches and pains. You know how bad my back and hands have been hurting from all the hair I've been doing. Plus, it's one free session for each new customer."

"If you insist... Just—" She pauses. "Call me after, okay? I want to hear all about how you screamed while getting in that bath because you're afraid of sinking under the water." More laughter echoes throughout my car.

"You really can be a bitch sometimes, you know that? It's not my fault I'm afraid of swimming."

"Whose is it, then?" Thea questions.

Turning off the car, I grab my purse and ready myself to get out. "Coach Dicky. My mother should've known he'd be a problem with a last name like that. Listen, I've gotta go."

She clears her throat. "I just love teasing you, Wren. But for real, enjoy yourself, and call me when you're done."

With a click, I exit the car and start my walk down the block toward the new relaxation Dyv'i bath spa in town. There are aliens known as the Wa'gōah that are composed of foreign water-based atoms. They are able to remove the atoms from their bodies and transfer them to water, which increases its buoyancy and adds restorative properties. Not only do I want to ease my cosmetology aches and pains, I'd also like to make it a goal to conquer my fear of going underwater someday. Maybe this is where I can start.

It's not like I can't shower or anything. It's just swimming and going under that scare the piss right out of me.

Hence why I'm giving—I stare up at the storefront, confirming the name—Spa'Wa a try.

A bell dings as I enter the spa and walk through a cloud of relaxing essential oils pumping throughout the space. Mmm. Eucalyptus, I think.

Walking toward the check-in desk, I smile at the array of fountains for sale—all shapes, sizes, and colors—scattered along tables, as well as the floor along the perimeter of the room.

There's a floor-to-ceiling waterfall-like fountain behind the desk, where an absolutely gorgeous alien male stands, checking in another customer.

With his attention on someone else, I take the time to stare, noting his light-blue skin covered in white, ripple-like tattoos. The sun dances through the front window, bouncing off his aquamarine eyes as he reaches up to run his hand through his short curls that are an incredibly deep blue—so dark, it makes me think of the deepest parts of the ocean.

Yikes. Don't want to get too far in with those thoughts. I'll freak myself out before I even get in one of these baths. On the other hand, I've got to prepare to flirt. Can't miss a chance with a hot alien; not when Thea got so lucky with Kiran. I mean, who doesn't want to buy a random dick plant from a greenhouse and have it help you find your fated mate? I'd give anything for it to be that easy for me.

Someday... That's what I keep telling myself. Someday, someone is going to find me, and I'm going to love them with all I have.

"Can I help you?" a baritone voice with a very sexy accent similar to Idris Elba—*yum*—jolts me from my daydream. It's coming from the gorgeous Dyv'i behind the counter—the one donning a suddenly crabby look.

Reaching up, I push some of my hair behind my ear as I approach the desk. "Hi. My name is Wren. I made an appointment for nine."

The male huffs and begins scrolling through his computer, his eyes scanning back and forth across the screen. Meanwhile, I try to ignore his grumpy demeanor and instead scan his beard of short stubble, wondering how it'd feel rubbing along my inner thighs.

He clicks the mouse. "Here we are. Wren Gaines?"

I nod. "Tha—"

GUSH!

A mini geyser of water shoots up into the air beside me, sending droplets of water all over my face. "Ah!" I scream, taken by surprise.

Within seconds, the water dies down, and I draw my eyes to my right, desperate to find the culprit of my embarrassment, as the male utters out a slew of apologies in a gruff voice.

But all I find is...

I point at a table-top fountain perched on the welcome counter, water now dribbling from its...head? "Is that—a penis?"

CHAPTER TWO

ALIOTH

Great... The most gorgeous woman I've ever seen just happens to stroll in and get drenched by what she can obviously tell is a phallus-shaped fountain. I probably look like a freak, having something like that in the welcome area of my spa, perched directly atop my desk.

Glancing between the beautiful blonde before me and that stupid fucking fountain—that's been collecting dust for the last five years—I reach for a towel and offer it to her, knowing it's a bit unnecessary, seeing as she'll be getting wet in one of our restorative baths shortly.

"Shit! I mean, crap! Ms. Gaines, I am so sorry." I grab another towel and start wiping down the ledge and my computer. "Or, Mrs. I—"

She swipes the towel over her face, and it's then that I notice there's not a lick of smudged makeup left in its wake. You'd be surprised how many people come in here with some sort of makeup on, which only ends up getting in the water and smearing all over their faces.

Not Wren Gaines, though. No. She came in with a bare face, and it's breathtakingly perfect.

"It's Miss, actually. Never married, single, and thirty, as of today, if you're wondering." An angelic chuckle falls from her mouth. "And it's okay. I'm about to get in the bath, anyway. What I'm really waiting for is your answer to my question." She purses her lips out with a hint of attitude.

I can't help but roll my eyes as I bite back a smirk, because I can only guess what her reaction might be.

My hand wraps around the base of the now-working fountain as I drag it in between us. "As you can tell, it very much is a phallus fountain, one I inherited from back home. It's finally working, apparently."

Wren cocks her head. "*Finally* working?"

"Yeah. I've changed out the water reservoir every single day since I received it, and never has the water actually come out. Today must be my lucky day."

Her smile widens so far, the rays of sunshine peeking through the windows sparkle off of her teeth, drawing attention to the slightly crooked front tooth that just barely covers the inner corner of the one next to it. It's fucking adorable.

She reaches a finger out to touch the water spilling from the tip of the fountain, and my dick grows hard. "It's strange—"

"Because it's shaped like a penis?" I question.

She shakes her head. "No. I decided that my thirties were going to be a decade of change for me literally this morning. Maybe this is a sign?" Her fingers travel to her temple as her gaze seems to drift off somewhere for a second, her next words growing quiet. "But a dick fountain is going to prove that to me? Am I crazy?"

She'd be shocked to know the coincidence of all of this...

Reaching over the counter, I use my pointer finger to bring her gaze back to mine. "Everything okay?"

Wren nods. "Yeah, sorry about that. I have a habit of getting in my head a little too much."

"That's all right. Are you all ready for your bath?"

"Ready!" she answers, a little too eagerly, her voice cutting out a bit as she pulls the collar of her shirt away from her neck.

Once I've got Wren all set up in the bath room, I'm halfway out the door, saying, "Let me know if you need anything," when she stops me with a tug on the doorknob.

"Wait!" she half-yells, her eyes trained on the bath. "I'm scared..."

I study her with a tilt of my head. "Of the bath? I promise there's nothing in there that could hurt you."

Wren shakes her head. "It's not that. It's—Well... I'm afraid of the water. What if I get so relaxed that I fall asleep and slip under the water and drown?"

A chuckle falls from my lips as I slip back into the room. "The buoyancy in these baths keeps you afloat. You won't slip under and drown."

"What if I flip over and drown that way?"

I sigh. "Well, your body would wake you up. The mind is a powerful thing, and no matter the cost, your instincts will do anything to keep you alive. Trust me, it would be a reflex for you to wake up."

She hugs herself and rubs the arms of the blue robe provided to each client.

Moving in front of her, I bend until her eyes find mine and rise with me. "Is everything okay, Miss Gaines?"

"Wren," she corrects. "You can call me Wren."

My eyes trail the bob of a swallow down her throat. "What's all this about, *Wren*?"

"I'm afraid of water. I don't like to swim, and when I do, I *refuse* to go under. Not a fan of baths, either. Being splashed in the face even bothers me…"

Guilt settles heavy in my stomach, because my stupid fucking fountain probably triggered all of this…

The very fountain that just alerted me to the fact that I just met the one I was destined to find on this planet.

My mate.

CHAPTER THREE

WREN

"I'm sorry," the seriously hot male whispers to me.

I tilt my head at him, forcing myself to use *anything* as a distraction. As much as I want to try out this pod, I am dreading getting in that water... "What's your name?"

His face shows no emotion whatsoever. "Um, Alioth."

"*Alioth*?" I repeat, and he nods. "That's an interesting name for an interesting alien."

"Thank you, I think?"

Laughter bursts from my lips, and a second later, I'm doubled over in a fit of what I can only describe as a nervous laugh attack.

I'm not sure if it's in worry or fear, but Alioth takes a few slow, carefully measured steps toward the door before I hear it creak open. "Miss... Wren, why don't we reschedule? It seems like you're very nervous about this, and I think everything got off to a *surprising* start."

"Surprising?" I chuckle. "Because your penis basically cumshot its load all over me? I mean, it did catch me a little off guard."

Wiping the tears from my face, I reopen my eyes and lock onto a petite old woman quite literally clutching her pearls in the doorway of the room we're in.

"Alioth?" she gasps.

The blue hunk grunts at the woman as he rests his hand on her shoulder. "Apologies, Mrs. Berrycloth. You can have a free bath session on me. Call me tomorrow so we can schedule it."

With a curt nod, she scurries away from us and out the door in record time, judging by the chime of the bells on the entrance.

Alioth huffs as he levels me with an almost accusatory stare.

Now it's my turn to gasp as I fling a hand to my heart. "What are you staring at *me* for?"

"Did you have to say *my penis cumshot its load on you*? That's not even what happened."

"Is too!" I argue.

"Is not!"

Hands to my hips, I puff out my chest at the sexy male and finish the childish argument. "Just because it's a fountain made of stone doesn't mean it's not a penis! It's not my fault that Lady Berrycloth can't handle embellishments. Now, are you going to help me get into this bath or what?"

It took approximately fifteen minutes for Alioth to help me get into the tub because of my squeals and twitches, but his calming voice and soothing touch helped get me onto my back, where he is now cradling me in his arms to keep me afloat. His grumpy exterior has also partially melted away.

How I managed to convince this sexy male of a water alien into treating me like a baby at its first swim lesson is beyond me. Then again, I feel like I can be pretty damn convincing.

Unfortunately, it's hard for me to relax, because I haven't tried floating on my back, nor have I been in a tub, since I was a child. Sure, the water in this bath only comes up to my knees while standing, but lying on my back? Well, that means I could definitely drown.

Yeah, that's right. Drown.

"I have to talk," I announce to Alioth, who's holding me up in the bath rather than working the counter of his own spa. "Do you have time?"

His sigh of warm breath blows across my face before he clears his throat. "My assistant, Raine, is out there. So, I *suppose* I have time. What would you like to talk about?"

I startle, white-knuckling both sides of the tub that I'm able to reach. For what reason, I don't know.

"Ummm…" I use my special superpower of being able to talk about literally anything to my advantage. "How many fearful people have you helped support in one of these Dyv'i baths?"

A few beats of silence pass before he grunts. "None."

"Really?" I half open my eye closest to him and assess his face. Annoyance. That's the look he dons. "That's kinda odd, isn't it?"

"The opposite, actually. You seem to be the *rarity*." He says rarity like there's some hidden meaning behind it.

I cross my arms, splashing some water that makes me go rigid, and performing an involuntary Kegel out of fear. "I'll pretend your tone holds zero offense. And I'll change the subject to deter you from further hurting my feelings by telling you that my best friend is married to a Dyv'i."

Alioth's fingers twitch against me, and I swear the feeling sweeps through every part of my body, landing directly on my clit. Squeezing my legs together, I play it off as if I have an itch on my ankle.

How is it possible that I'm getting turned on while in one of the most terrifying situations of my life?

CHAPTER FOUR

ALIOTH

It takes a second for me to register what Wren just told me, because her appetizing fucking arousal is permeating my nose as if it's all the surrounding air is comprised of.

I never should've gotten myself in this position. I should've just canceled this appointment and sent her on her merry way. But how could I refuse my mate, knowing it might take away my chance of keeping her?

And how, in the name of galaxies, have I been destined for a mate who is terrified of the very element I'm connected to?

This can't work. I mean, how could it?

I'm in love with the thing she fears most...

"Did you hear me?" my blonde beauty asks.

I rouse, raking her from head-to-toe while her eyes remain closed. "Yes. That's...interesting. What subspecies?"

"Ced'oh. His name is Kiran. Do you know him? Big, green dude? Owns a greenhouse? Has this penis plant that apparently helped him find my best friend? Thea, she's great. Says alien sex is literally out of this world." She releases a dreamy sigh. "That pun was fully intended, by the way."

I can't help but roll my eyes. "First of all, no, I don't know this Kiran dude. Second, this is *supposed* to be relaxing. That means no talking."

Wren clicks her tongue. "Yeahhhh. Water isn't relaxing to me, as you might have noticed. So, I'd rather talk—at least for this first time. And plus, it helps to have you in here. Why wouldn't I talk to someone that's in here with me? Even *you* need a distraction."

"From what?"

"Checking me out."

My face warms. "Excuse me?"

"I can feel your stare, Alioth. It's a gift."

Do human women have superpowers? I remember reading about *Wonder Woman* once, but I thought she was make believe? I don't recall gifted powers being part of *Welcome to Earth 101*.

Super powers or not, Wren isn't wrong about my staring. I try to keep my gaze focused elsewhere for the rest of the session.

Wren finally quiets down after forty-five minutes, but we still have an hour left, and even though I love being in the water, I'm fucking sick of this. Would I give anything to spend all the time in the world with my mate? Obviously. But not like this. I'd rather be rubbing my hands along her perfect body, removing her wetsuit, and pulling her lower half beneath the water so I can sheath my coc—"What are you doing?" Wren yelps as her body goes rigid.

My distraction has cost me, because I didn't realize how low my arms were dropping, accidentally lowering Wren deeper into the water, which has obviously caused a panic.

Before I can answer, both of her hands reach out for safety. One clutches the side of the bath, and the other, in a desperate search to grab on to anything, grabs my motherfucking nose.

"Ow!" I yell.

"Sorry! I just...got scared."

I harumph as she settles back into my hold, her breathing finally leveling back out.

The rest of our time is spent with Wren babbling about random topics and asking the most off-the-wall questions. All the while, I continue with my usual grunts, gruffs, and sighs. Small talk has never been my thing. Then again, others really haven't been either...

Straightening my legs, I lift her out of the water and into the air, where I cradle her against my chest and exit the tub. "Time's up, Miss Gaines. Are you sure you'd still like to consider a membership?"

I set her on her feet, and she grabs a towel from the shelf on the wall and begins mopping up the water collecting at her feet.

"Again, I'm sorry. Ya know, for grabbing your nose when I got a little scared and all..."

Her body deflates as she stares up at me with eyes so broken, I feel like I'm watching one of those animal shelter commercials, and it nearly rips me in two. Sad animals can tear apart just about anyone, but seeing my mate sad? The one I'm destined to spend the rest of my days with? I don't know if it's something I can possibly recover from.

I bend down and reach for her hand, grasping it in mine. "Hey, hey. It's okay. I apologize for startling you. Why don't you head to the washroom at the end of the hallway to dry off and get changed? I'll meet you up front."

She nods as she backs away to grab her things and leave the room, her shoulders more hunched than they were when she entered my shop.

Shit... She voiced her fears with me; trusted me with her vulnerability. I should've been paying attention. But I guess I was a bit blindsided. I had basically accepted I'd never find my mate. And now that I have, how the fuck am I supposed to make it work when she's this afraid of water? I mean, I have a pool in my damn house. Will just the sight of it scare her away?

This seems like a doomed situation...

As I spread my hands wide, my palms facing the ground, I breathe in deep through my nose and force the droplets of water to rise and accumulate until they're a large, flowy ball that I grasp on to and toss back in to join the rest of the bath water.

Then I head toward the check-in area, dreading the fact that my mate might take me up on my word and never return.

What then?

CHAPTER FIVE

WREN

"Hello?" Thea answers in a chipper tone, probably hopeful that everything here today was a success.

I cup my hand around where my mouth meets the speaker and whisper, "Are you at home?"

"Yes? Why are we whispering?"

I chuff. "Because I'm *beyond* humiliated. Can I come over?"

"Of course. Are you all right?" Concern blankets her tone, and I can hear her perk up by the creak of whatever chair she's sitting in.

Thea may own her dream flight-style restaurant, but most of her work is done from the comfort of her own home, which she prefers. Her alien mate, Kiran, built her a gorgeous in-home office for her to work in while he goes to work at his year-round greenhouse every day.

They got together after Thea bought his mate-attractor plant he had on display at Cēd, and though it took some time and convincing, they're literally the happiest couple I know. They even have plans to get married within the next year!

"Okay. I'll be there in thirty."

After grabbing my bag and shoving my phone inside my pants pocket, I take a cleansing breath and head back out to the lobby in search of Alioth, so I can apologize once again for the absolute disaster I created for him.

Instead, I'm greeted by a gorgeous human woman with hair so black, everything else in the room pales in comparison. Her warm, dark gaze slips over to meet mine, and she offers me a wide grin from behind the counter.

"Hello, Miss Gaines. Alioth will be out momentarily. He requested I ask you to wait for him before leaving. My name is Raine."

I hold out my hand to shake hers. "You can call me Wren. Your name is beautiful and very fitting for working here."

She throws her head back with a boisterous laugh. "I tease Alioth sometimes by saying that's the sole reason he hired me. Someone has to be the mascot around here."

Oh, I fucking love her. And I wonder if Alioth loves her, too. Like, as more than an employee and friend. Maybe they're together.

That would mean one of my chances at finding my own alien mate might possibly be down the drain.

No. Oh, fuck no. Water jokes are *not* allowed, not even from me.

"Alioth!" Raine calls. "Don't leave Miss Gaines waiting out here all day. I've got shit to do, grumpy pants." She shoots me another bright smile before leaving the room, calling over her shoulder, "It was nice to meet you, Wren. I hope to see you again."

Thankful she's not looking right at me, I blink a few times to clear any possibility of tears. I can't believe my fear of water messed all of this up so badly...

Beads clink together as Alioth reappears from the back with a huff, his eyes sweeping the room for Raine, I'm guessing. "Sorry about that, Wren."

His gaze flits between me and that damn penis fountain that's still running. It feels like it's mocking me and my heinous experience. I mean, who asks a spa owner to hold them in a bath?

"No problem. It's me who should be apologizing. Alioth, I— I did not mean to do that, and I'm sorry for the trouble I've caused here." I move even closer to the counter but remain a few inches away from the stupid-ass fountain. "What can I do to qualify for a membership? That's the first time I've felt somewhat safe in water that deep. I think continuous exposure might help me."

He laughs, and it's a deep, steady one that gives me chills. "I won't turn you away. If you'd like to return and try again, you're welcome to do so. Although, I don't think it's wise for us to be put in the same predicament as today, but I could fill the tub you use with much less water than was in there. That might help."

I offer a small smile, trying not to stare too long into his crystalline eyes or at his Malibu blue skin. "I'll think about it, if that's okay, but there's just one more thing I'd like to do before I go."

"What's that?"

Taking slow, shimmying side steps, I position myself in front of the penis fountain, trying to keep my eyes open, but they're twitching so bad, I feel like I'm staring down the puff machine at the eye doctor.

With a penny I pulled from my purse grasped in my hands, I close my eyes at the same time the beads clink again, signaling me to the possibility that Raine is now part of my audience.

Alioth releases a grunt, and they begin whisper-arguing between themselves in words so hushed I can't hear them over my mentally whispered wishes. And when I open my eyes and toss the penny into the moat of water surrounding the dick statue in the middle, Alioth grows quiet, while Raine does everything she can to suppress the giggle dancing along her shaking lips.

"What?" I question, shifting my eyes between them both.

Raine works hard to school her features before saying, "That's not a wish fountain..."

"A *what*?" Alioth asks.

"Listen here, old man trapped in a hot alien body," I start. "There are things called wish fountains here on Earth. People sometimes make a wish and toss a penny into the water, hoping it'll come true."

He quirks a brow at me. "And what did you wish for?"

Raine all but lunges over the counter, smacking her hand to my mouth. "Wishes aren't supposed to be told!"

Meanwhile, I stand there, staring at the hot blue male with a stranger's hand clasped over my mouth and the continuous trickle of the fountain ringing in my ears. I just threw a penny into a phallus-shaped fountain that is *not* a wishing well. My thirties are definitely not off to the best of starts, I'd say.

"Can you remove your hand and allow Wren to speak for herself, Raine?" Alioth sneers, crossing his arms over his strong chest. "Oh my God! I'm so sorry." Raine's face is pained as she frees my mouth and wipes her hand on her shirt.

I shake my head, starting to wonder if I'm in some freaky alternative reality or something. Maybe I did drown, and this is my personal hell—stuck in a loop of the longest day ever at a business dedicated to water.

Which is why I probably should ruin my wish. It'd definitely lead to even more nightmares...

"I wished for a redo at swimming lessons."

CHAPTER SIX

ALIOTH

Swimming lessons? My mate threw a penny into the fountain that just so happens to be an exact replica of my...*member* and wished for a redo at swimming lessons? I'd hope she'd wish for a night with me.

Raine gasps. "There's a super hot new lifeguard that works at the local recreation center. Comes from a family of billionaires or something, so he offers lessons on the side for fun because he loves swimming."

Anger courses through my veins. No way in hell is the woman meant for me taking swim lessons from some hotshot billionaire.

I growl in Raine's direction, feeling like an utter beast, and she squints at me and my noise of a response. She doesn't take my shit. Ever.

Ignoring her, I turn back to Wren. "I can teach you to swim. There's no being more qualified than a Wa'gōah."

The heat of Raine's stare warms my cheek closest to her. "Since when do you—"

I cut her off. "I've been playing around with the idea, and this is something I'd love to help you with, Wren. Think of it as a deal. You allow me to practice teaching someone how to swim, and I'll give you free spa offerings."

Wren mulls it over, chewing on the inside of her cheek while Raine throws up her hands and leaves the room with a whispered, *"This is real fucking rich."*

"Is she okay?" my blonde goddess asks, unease leaking from her staccato-like movements.

Desperate for her to agree to my proposal, I lean over the counter, inches from her face. "What do you say, Wren?"

Her gaze slowly wanders from my eyes to my mouth and back again while a rush of her delicious scent wafts into my nose, and it takes all I have *not* to close my eyes and groan while she's staring up at me.

"I— Um... I don't know. I wouldn't want to put you through what I already did today."

I huff. "Wren, you just made a wish for a redo at swimming lessons, right?"

She nods.

"Well, I'm offering you my services. Now... What do you say, darling?"

Her eyes widen at the term of endearment, and I make a mental note. I guess this older guy still has it.

She runs a hand down her face. "Fine. When do we start?"

"When do you want to start?"

Her eyes drop to the floor as she silently mulls through what I'm assuming is her schedule. "I have a full day at the salon tomorrow and Wednesday, but what about Thursday? I don't go in until the afternoon."

"Salon?" I quirk a brow.

Wren smiles. "I'm a hairdresser. If you ever need a haircut, I'm your girl. I'd be happy to offer my services in exchange for yours."

I can't help the smirk that pulls up at the corner of my mouth. "Services, huh?"

A blush crawls up her cheeks, and suddenly, I feel like a fucking pervert.

"Sorry," I rush out. "I didn't mean it like that." Even though I did. "Thursday will work. If you want to get to my place around 10 a.m., we can swim for an hour, and then you can do what you need to in order to get ready for work."

"Your place?"

I nod. "Is that okay?"

She shrugs. "I mean, yeah. I just didn't anticipate you having a pool at your house that we could use in October. Ya know, Michigan weather and all..."

"It's indoors, actually," I tell her as I write down my address and phone number before handing her the scrap of paper. "But anyway, I should get back to work. I'll see you in a few days."

My beautiful blonde waves at me before turning around and sauntering those perfect hips toward the exit. "Bye, Alioth. Sorry about everything! And also, thank you for the...lessons. Tell Raine I said goodbye, too, please."

"No worries. See you Thursday, *darling*."

The accentuation of the word has her tripping on air for a brief second before she recovers and scurries out of the spa.

"Soooo, are these swimming lessons also dates, or what?" Raine asks. "And since when does your grumpy attitude soften at the sight of a hot blonde?"

The two of us are cleaning the giant floor-to-ceiling windows that face the quaint downtown street, and I can't help but regret asking her to help me.

"No, Raine. They're not. And I'm always grumpy, but she's a customer."

She scoffs. "A customer, huh? Alioth, I saw the way you looked at her. Not to mention, I didn't know we held clients in the tubs now? When did that perk get added to our list of services? I'll make sure to add it to the website."

"Don't you dare," I order. "I already told her it will not happen again. I felt bad for the poor girl. She was too scared to even float on her back without someone there."

"*Girl*? You make her sound like she's a teenager. She's a *woman*, Alioth. And it's okay to be attracted to her. She's fucking gorgeous."

If only she knew...

As a species, each of our subspecies is gifted something meant to either attract our mate, or alert us to the fact that we found them. It's something we don't disclose, just like the fact that we transform into our true form during intercourse. We don't even know the specific gifts for each subspecies; only our own. It's easier to keep secrets you don't know, I suppose.

Raine is aware of my fountain, knows that it is a gift from home, but doesn't know what it's for. Maybe that's something I can tell her about. Maybe she could help me with the Wren situation.

"I'm well aware, Raine. I have eyes, for God's sake."

She faces me, pushing her bouncy, thick curls over her shoulders. "So, what are you going to do?"

I slowly breathe in and back out before leveling my gaze on her and dragging a hand down my face with a long groan at her incessant questioning. "See where things go?"

With a final scrub of the window, Raine climbs down her stepladder. "Well, if you ever need my help, or want to talk things out, you know where to find me. You deserve to find someone, old man."

"I'm not old!" I holler after her.

She chuckles. "You're older than me! That means you're *old*!"

What does she know? Forty in human years isn't old... Especially considering the Dyv'i can live well into the hundreds. But then again, she and Wren seem to be the same age, so what if Wren thinks I'm too old for her? She called me an old man. Maybe that means she's already counting me out.

That could be a predicament, seeing as we're fated to be together. If she wants to be, that is...

CHAPTER SEVEN

WREN

"Wait, wait, wait, wait, *waitttttt* a damn minute. What do you mean, the hot blue alien *held you* in the bathtub?" Thea asks, staring at me with wide eyes.

I roll my eyes. "It's not a bathtub, Thea. It is bigger than that, and filled with water from Dyv'iëdus. And he didn't *hold* me." I form quotation marks with my fingers and then go on to share the story all over again.

Thea falls back onto the couch in a fit of laughter. "A penis fountain—" She gasps. "Sprayed you—" Another gasp. "And then you—" A third gasp. "Threw a penny—"

"All right, that's e-fucking-nough!" I cut her off, because if I have to hear one more gasp as she works through my horror of an experience, I'm going to pull a Raine and clap my hand over her mouth. "Yes. All those things happened, Thea. You're supposed to be helping me, not making fun of me!"

She wipes the tears from below her eyes. "I'm not making fun of you, Wrenny, I just... Well... I would laugh if that had happened to me. Instead, I just kept breaking off Willy's, well, *willy*!"

Willy is the plant Thea bought from Kiran's greenhouse, which then led to them falling in love. Oh, and Willy just so happens to be a plant that is *penis* shaped. Go figure! What is it with the Dyv'i and dicks?

Ha. Double D.

Dragging my hands down my face, I huff out a breath of air. "I mean, don't get me wrong, I do find it hilarious because it would only happen to us, but I need advice on hot aliens. Forget all of that for right now and help me!"

The front door of Thea's house creaks open, and her fiancé, Kiran, walks through, his towering frame and sage-green skin catching my eye. My best friend is one lucky girl.

I lean closer and whisper in her ear, "You need to help me snag one of *those*." My finger is still pointing at Kiran when his eyes land on us.

"Hi, sweet girl. Hey, Wren," he greets. "Why do you both look like you're causing trouble?"

Thea shrugs and then word vomits. "Wren tried that Dyv'i bath spa, got sprayed by a penis fountain, had a hot blue alien help her float, and then made a wish on said penis fountain!" Her laughter takes over again, and she puts a hand to her stomach as I give Kiran a look with a tight-lipped grin.

He shakes his head at me. "She just can't help herself, can she?"

I shake my head. "Nope. Not at all."

Kiran kicks off his work boots and heads for us, planting a kiss on top of Thea's head before sitting beside her on the couch. "While Thea works through this laughing fit, why don't you start from the beginning again? If you don't mind sharing the story with me."

So I do. And I can't help but notice the way Thea and Kiran's heads whip toward each other each time I mention the phallic fountain, like there's something I'm missing.

"What?"

Thea's eyes shift from left to right. "What do you mean, *what*?"

I scrunch my eyebrows and jut out my head in her direction. "Are one of you going to tell me why you seem so taken aback by the fountain?"

It's Kiran who pipes up first. "It's just an odd item to have on display in a place of business."

"And Willy wasn't?"

Thea places her hand on my knee. "Two different types of items, babe. Can't compare a growing plant with something made of stone. I wouldn't read too much into it, but if you do want to see if something could happen between you and Alioth, I think you should ask him to dinner as a thank-you for lessons, or maybe even as an apology for what happened. *Oooo*, or offer him haircuts in exchange!"

"That was actually the exact exchange offer I gave him…" I told her, already imagining a big, bulky Alioth sitting in my chair at the salon. Maybe I should invest in a bigger chair to accommodate his height. I already have a very wide chair to comfortably fit all sizes, because no one should feel uncomfortable and squished when sitting to get their hair done for possibly hours. But height? I guess I've never encountered anyone near Kiran's height before.

"But neither of you think I should look into the penis fountain more? I know you said the plant was what led you to your mate, Thea. Maybe the fountain is mine."

Tongue in cheek, Thea seems at a loss for words before turning to her mate. "Care to weigh in, Kiran?"

He clears his throat. "Every Dyv'i subspecies differs from each other, not only the elements and other things they're connected with, but also the way they find their mates. We do not share the customs of our own with one another. I have no idea what the Wa'gōah do to find their fated mates. I'm sorry."

I shrug, knowing it's just my luck. But that's okay. Maybe Alioth's kind are ones that grow to love one another. Maybe he doesn't have a mate-attractor at all.

But damn, it'd be nice if he did.

CHAPTER EIGHT

ALIOTH

The last few days have passed by excruciatingly slow, and of course, now that Thursday has arrived, time is flying by, and I'm getting nervous.

Yeah. Me, a forty-year-old alien from another planet, is nervous about giving swim lessons to his fated mate.

Why? Well, to put it simply—being around her makes me nervous. What if we both get turned on and I try to make a move without thinking? What if she gets scared again and doesn't want to continue?

"Hello?" a voice calls. "*Alioth*!"

I stir from my trance and focus on Raine's face, which is directly in front of me. "Jeez. What is it, Raine?"

She holds up my phone. "Your alarm has been going off for like two minutes. It's time for you to go and teach swimming lessons to your *crush*." The way she accentuates the last word grinds on my nerves.

With a hand to my temple, I close my eyes in disbelief. I'm apparently never going to live this down. "I can't stand to be around you any longer. Don't forget to set the alarm when you leave," I say, grabbing my backpack from behind the counter and beelining for the front door.

"Make sure to wear your banana hammock!"

Instead of letting the door slowly fall closed, I slam it behind me, not wanting the hustle and bustle of the storefront sidewalk to hear her yells. What is she even talking about, anyway?

"Hey, Google. What is a banana hammock?"

Wren: ETA is in five minutes.

I shoot her a thumbs-up and head for the door, pulling a T-shirt on as I go, and adjust my swim trunks. No banana hammocks for me after what Google showed me. Why the hell would anyone want to wear one of those?

Especially if you're teaching a hot chick how to swim. My hard-on would probably take her eye out. I can already picture rushing her to the hospital and having to explain that her blurred vision was caused by a boner to the eye. Next thing you know, our story would wind up on one of those television shows about what crazy things led to an emergency room visit.

I'm good on all that.

KNOCK. KNOCK. KNOCK.

I take a deep breath, steadying my nerves before opening the door. My heart stops.

Wren stands before me in a sunshine yellow one-piece that hugs every part of her perfect body, like it was specifically designed for her. Her platinum-blonde hair is tied up in a messy bun on top of her head, and a sheer cover-up is wrapped and knotted around her waist.

Tattoos stretch along the length of one of her legs, and I swear to God, I could lick every inch with my tongue and it still wouldn't be enough. My mate is fucking hot.

"Are you going to let me in? Or keep staring?"

Dropping my eyes to the floor, I step aside and wave her in. "I'm sorry. I didn't mean to stare."

She chuckles. "Yes, you did, and that's okay. I was staring at you, too. You just didn't notice because of your wandering eyes."

Hm. My girl's got spunk. Seems to me like that bravery could pay off in dirty talk.

Nope. Get that thought out of your head right now, Alioth, or your hard dick will be showing Wren the way to the pool instead of your finger.

"Pool's this way," I announce, pointing toward the back of the house. With my finger, just for the record.

Wren lets out a short whistle. "Your house is gorgeous. Do I get a tour?"

Thankfully, she can't see the smirk that pulls up at the corner of my mouth since she's behind me, because I'm going to use this to my advantage. "How about you earn it, *darling*?"

CHAPTER NINE

WREN

There he goes with that *darling* again in that sexy accent of his. I wonder if other Dyv'i subspecies have different accents, because Kiran seems to have one just like ours here in the Upper Midwest...

My thoughts come to an abrupt halt as we enter the indoor pool area. I swear I just walked into a celebrity's house.

Windows cover every wall and even the ceiling, granting the space complete visual access to outside weather. It's a tad cloudy today, but that's all right, because the thick expanse of autumn trees makes for the perfect background.

Stone tile flooring stretches around the length of the pool. Various lounge chairs, a dining table, a bar, and a raised hot tub are peppered throughout the room.

"Holy shitballs!" I exclaim.

Alioth spins toward me, a disgusted frown pulling down at the corners of his mouth. "I hope that doesn't mean you have balls of shit in your bathing suit, because that would mean you definitely can't swim in my pool today."

I hold up my hands at him, cackling. "No. No. It doesn't mean that at all. I mean, *ew*. Holy shitballs is just a phrase I use. It's like saying holy shit."

"Okay?" His head twitches slightly. "Anyway, let's get started, shall we?"

Alioth's long, blue, toned arm reaches up and over his head to grab on to the middle upper back of his T-shirt collar, and then he tugs it off in that way all the hot guys in movies do, leaving his dark curls shimmying in its wake. *Hot damn*, this male is fine.

His back is covered in designs I'm uncertain about. It's hard to tell if they're tattoos made of actual ink, or if they're a natural part of his skin. They range in color from the very light white, similar to what you see at the bottom of a pool when sunlight shines in, to navy blue, like his luscious locks.

I so badly want to run my finger over them, followed by my tongue. I bet he is fabulous in bed.

Not wasting any time, Alioth hurries down the steps into the pool, and when he turns to face me, I notice his eyes have taken on a bright aquamarine that resembles the light-blue ripples flowing away from his body.

"Your eyes glow?"

He shakes his head at me and holds out his hands. "Please don't ask questions I'm not ready to answer, Wren. Come here."

My vagina doesn't stand a chance...

Not only do I have a hot, blue, shirtless alien male standing in the water, but add in his tattoos, thick curls, facial scruff, deep, commanding voice, and older age, and my bathing suit might slip off *accidentally*. That happens, right?

As I tug off my cover-up, I actually consider asking him to turn around so I can attempt to mop up the wetness pooling between my thighs, but it doesn't seem like his stare will break, so instead, I keep my eyes locked on his, throw the fabric to the ground, and basically waddle over to the edge of the pool.

Alioth clears his throat before forcing down what seems like a hard swallow as he gazes up at me, breathing in slowly and deeply. "We don't have all day, Wren." His tone is a lot friendlier than the one he seems to use with everyone at his job. And damn, the way he's eyeing me says that he wishes we *did* have all day together. And I can't say I disagree...

I nod, suddenly even more scared of the water, which I didn't think was possible. How am I supposed to try to score this guy when we're trying to connect over the very thing that scares me most? And how the fuck am I so incredibly horny, yet absolutely petrified?

Know what would help? An orgasm.

No. Get that out of your head, Wren. That is *so* inappropriate.

It's frowned upon to sleep with someone before you're in a relationship, so I hear. Thanks, *Mom...*

Then again, Thea and Kiran fell in love, and they started off as a one-night stand.

Besides, I'm thirty fucking years old! If I want my swim instructor to give me an orgasm to calm me down, I can do that. I mean, if he wants to, that is. I'm not going to grab the man by his hair and slam his face into my cooch or anything. Although, that'd be pretty great.

"You going to stand there daydreaming all day, or are you going to join me?"

I swallow down my fantasies and nod. I think I can get down with this teasing side of Alioth. "No. I'm ready. I think," I mutter as I dip a toe in. "Wait. No. Maybe I'm not."

A gruff huff escapes Alioth's lips as he climbs back up the stairs and towers over me, breathing heavily with those electrifying eyes.

"What are you doin—"

Before I can finish, he has me swept up in his arms in a tight embrace, and I can't help but screech.

"Wait! Please don't throw me in! I can do it!!!"

"Throw you in?" he questions, his brows scrunching tensely.

I hold tight to his shoulders, trembling. "Yeah. That's what Coach Dicky did to all of us growing up."

He shakes his head, and his jaw ticks. "That's a barbaric way to teach you to swim. I need you to calm down, Wren, darling. I would never do something like that to you, nor would I do something as ridiculous as that without asking, okay?"

I nod. "R-right. Okay."

Last time I was in water with Alioth, it was the first time I felt some calm when it came down to it. Which means I can totally feel that way again.

"Take a deep breath for me."

I do exactly as he says, numerous times, and slow my heartbeat the best I can.

"Good girl."

Oh, God. He did *not* just say that. Not helping, not helping, not helping at all.

"Now, may I carry you into the water?"

Trying to make light of the situation, I shoot him a wink. "Let's get wet, old man."

CHAPTER TEN

ALIOTH

If it weren't for her delicious arousal invading my nose, and the after-shocks of her fear trembling against my skin, I would've considered throwing her in.

Okay, not really. But seriously, what is up with everyone joking about my age lately? It must happen when you finally hit forty in human years. They must do it to everyone.

"Ha ha," I mock laugh. "Very funny."

Focused on the task at hand, I slowly and carefully take one step at a time into the water, never loosening my grip on Wren.

"You doing okay? We're halfway in. Am I good to go all the way?"

She laughs, and it's a delight to see her adorable overlapping teeth up close.

I quirk a brow at her. "What's so funny?"

"Ohhh, nothing, Alioth. Nothing I should say out loud, anyway."

Good to know both of our minds are in the gutter. It could make for a very interesting first lesson. Seeing as my cock is hard as fucking steel in my trunks right now, I don't want to comment for fear her filthy mouth will say something that causes an issue.

Dyv'i males are in humanoid form almost all the time, except for when we're most intimate with our mates. It's knowledge only shared with our partners, agreed upon by our kind once we landed here.

I've got to keep my shit together as much as possible. I can't risk transforming right in front of her...

Once we make it into the water, only half of her body is covered with the warm liquid, and we just stand there, holding on to each other.

A few minutes of silence pass before Wren finally speaks. "Okay. I think you can put me down now, but slowly—and by the edge so I can hold on to something." The last part flies out of her mouth at super-speed.

The request makes things more convenient, because I can let her down to my left instead of down my front, where she'd surely encounter my boner.

Ever so gently, I tilt inch by inch as she faces the perimeter and holds on to the stone ledge. Her feet drift closer and closer to the bottom, and she looks like she's about ready to climb out of the damn pool.

That is, before a moan escapes her mouth and she pushes up on the ledge.

"You doing okay?"

"Fuck," she whispers under her breath. "No!"

Another moan drifts past those perfect lips, and it takes everything in me not to come right then and there.

But in the next moment, Wren is thrashing, kicking me straight in the groin, and falling back against me.

Not wanting to have her slip under and possibly swallow some of the water, I ignore the pain and grasp at her the best I can, but one of my hands ends up grasping her pussy, and the other is on her tit.

"Don't drop me!"

I squeeze tighter, waiting for her limbs to still.

And they quickly do, but it's her pebbled nipple beneath my left hand and her pulsing, swollen cunt against my fingers that grab my attention.

I'm going to blow. That I'm sure of.

Wren moans again. "*Alioth...*" It's a breathy plea, and while I'm almost certain I can translate it on my own, I need her to use her words.

"What is it, darling? Use your words."

"I—uh—could use a little...help."

I breathe in her apple-scented hair. "With?"

She gently pushes at me, trying to escape my grasp. "Can you please let me go, so I can look at you when I ask?"

The groan I've been holding in rumbles deep in my chest as I lower her, making sure to avoid my still-present erection.

Awkwardly walking on her tiptoes, she holds my hands and turns to face me. Her face is flushed, and her eyes are heavy-lidded.

Then her eyes drift over her shoulder, to the edge of the pool. "The jet. It— It caught me by surprise, if you know what I mean."

So that's what happened. I'm assuming the pressure on her clit startled her. *Mmm.*

"Go on," I urge, desperate to discover where this conversation is going.

The tip of her tongue travels along the length of her bottom lip as her eyes travel between my chest and face. "Do you think you'd be able to help me, ya know, relax?"

One hand to her stomach, I walk her back until her body reaches the perimeter of the pool. She jumps and closes her eyes as the jet pelts against her back.

I can tell the distraction is helping, so I decide to see where this might go. This is for her. I'll do whatever she asks of me.

Caging her in between my arms, I lower my mouth to her ear. "Are you asking me to give you a yoga session? Or an orgasm?"

Her breath hitches. "The latter."

"With pleasure."

CHAPTER ELEVEN

WREN

Alioth's breath softly caresses the damp skin of my neck, making me shiver.

"Tell me what to do," I all but beg.

He nips at my earlobe before whispering, "Turn around."

And I do, trying to regain my composure, even though the jet is now flowing at my stomach. Any touch, be it water or hot alien male, is dancing over all of my erogenous zones, nearing me toward release with barely anything.

"Now," he starts, "close your eyes and trust me. I promise to only make you feel good."

I nod, allowing my eyes to follow instructions. For some odd rea-son, even though I've barely known this man for a week, I trust him. More than I ever trusted my swimming coach, that's for sure.

His powerful hands wander over my hips and behind my thighs before he lifts, tucking me into his chest with my knees pressed together. And before I can question *how* he plans to make me feel *good*, he wrenches my legs apart. The jet explodes against the material of my suit, right over my clit, like a fire hose at work. I squeal, taken by the sweetest surprise.

"You like that?" Alioth coos in my ear, moving me even closer to the edge where the pressure increases.

I twitch against him. "Fuck! Yes! Oh my God, Alioth. Do not *fucking* move."

Using his body as leverage, he manages to thrust my hips out, repeatedly, helping me ride the water, and damn... I'm so fucking close.

Alioth rubs his nose down the column of my neck before licking his way back up. "Are you going to come apart in my pool, Wren? Is the water getting you off, baby?"

Winding one of my arms over my head and around his neck, I sneak the other inside the top of my suit, pinching at one of my nipples. "I'm so close, Alioth. Keep going. Yes, right there. Yes!" I scream out my release as my body convulses against him, splashing sounds echoing around us in the enormous space, but he doesn't let go.

No.

Instead of releasing me, Alioth holds position, refusing to give my aching bud a break from the pressure.

"What are you doing?" I screech, uncertain if I should release my grips or hold on tighter. "Uhh." I moan. "I finished. You can put me—*fuck*—down."

He presses my knees to the siding of the pool, and the opening of the jet is even closer to my clit, the water at its most potent. "Not until you give me one more. Now, play with your tits, Wren. Show me what you look like when you come undone again so soon."

Don't have to ask me twice. The pressure. Oh my God, the pressure.

A second orgasm is already standing at the precipice, just waiting to jump, so I snake both of my arms beneath my suit top and play with my puckered nipples more.

"Right there, right there, right there. Oh, *yes*. Alioth, hurry up and lick my neck again. Maybe even—*mmm*. I'm there. I'm literally there. Bite me, damn it! Fuck!"

His teeth latch on to the side of my neck, and I erupt with a scream and a thrash. But he holds me there, letting me ride out the waves of pleasure as he licks away the pain of his bite.

"So beautiful when you come, my darling. Look at the way you used the water to get yourself off. I think you might not be as scared of it as you think you are."

While I come down from my post-orgasm high, Alioth stands behind me, pinning my body between his hard muscles and the hard stone of the pool's edge.

We say nothing for a few minutes, both lost in silence, and I'm sure in our heads over what just transpired between us.

I can't believe I asked him to do that. Okay, that's a fucking lie. I can. My big mouth has no problem whatsoever asking for what I want. But I can't believe he went along with it.

Although, I don't think anyone could deny the scorching hot fire sizzling between us since I arrived at his house. We have a connection, and I plan on doing everything I can to get him to explore it.

"You still awake back there?" I ask. "Because if so, I'd love to return the favor."

His groan is so low and deep and similar to a purr that I have to mentally give it my all to remain composed.

He takes a step away from me, giving me enough room to turn and face him, and even with his blue-colored skin, I can tell he is flushed with arousal.

Alioth's Adam's apple bobs with a swallow. "No. This was for you."

My eyebrows shoot upward. "You're telling me your cock doesn't want attention? Really, Alioth?"

He shakes his head.

"But—"

"We need to focus on your lessons. Please, Wren. Leave it be. I'm fine."

I shrug and reach for his arm. "Whatever you say. But just for the record, thank you. That was hot, and I feel sooo much better."

A proud smile tugs up at the corners of his mouth.

"So, what's next, coach?"

CHAPTER TWELVE

ALIOTH

"We're only working on two things today," I start, holding up two of my long fingers. "Walking the pool and splashing your face."

Wren quirks a brow at me. "Walking and splashing? How is that going to help?"

I cross my arms and level her with an unamused glare. "If you're so afraid of the water that I have to literally carry you in, we need to start with the basics. You should be able to walk around in the shallow end and splash your own face without having an issue. So"—I wave her away with my hand—"let's go."

My beautiful blonde mate walks along the perimeter of the pool, gripping the edge as she stares down at her feet and makes her way along the length of the shallow end. Every time my phone timer goes off, I have her splash her face a couple of times, so she expects what's coming.

And when we reach the length of our lesson time together, I help her out of the pool and into a towel, enthralled with the way she uses it to squeeze over her covered breasts to absorb all the moisture.

They're perfect. Utterly perfect, and the dream size for me.

Suddenly, I'm reminded of her two orgasms in the pool, how she got off from the water, how she couldn't stop playing with her nipples, and how she wanted me to bite her.

There's something about her asking me to mark her skin with my teeth that I can't get out of my head...

For fuck's sake. I'm getting hard again.

"Well, I have to get going so I can get to work. Next Thursday again?" she questions, those big, gorgeous brown eyes staring up at me.

I nod but have a strong desire to see her much sooner. "Would you like to join me for dinner tonight? And do you have any availability tomorrow for one of those haircuts you owe me for our first lesson?"

Her wide smile is purely wicked, followed by a playful lick before she rolls her lips. "Yes to dinner, and yes to the haircut. Text me the deets for tonight, and I'll do the same for time slots."

Then she traipses over to me, stands on her tiptoes, places a hand over my abs, and gives me a chaste kiss on the cheek. My body heats with desire.

"See ya later, Alioth. Pick a restaurant I can dress all sexy for, okay?"

Before I can answer, she's already gone, her retreat followed by the closing of the front door.

Wren is on her knees before me, her dark eyelashes fluttering as she slides her tightened fist over the length of my cock over and over again.

I grunt and groan, meeting her thrust for thrust as she works me over. "Fuck, baby. That's it. I need your mouth on me. Go on, open up," I beg her, desperate for more.

She moans as my tentacles play with her clit and dripping-wet cunt in tandem, then opens her mouth to me.

Ever so slowly, I slide between her lips as her tongue rubs side to side, and when I'm all the way in, she hollows out her cheeks and sucks as if she is sucking out my soul.

Wrapping her hair in my fist, I hold her there as I fuck her mouth. "Shit, darling. You suck me so good. I'm going to come in your mouth, okay? Is that what you want?"

Her head bobs up and down with a nod before she wraps her hands around my ass and picks up the pace on my shaft. I'm forced to release her hair and brace myself against the shower wall as she pulls me to the back of her throat, holding me there.

One of her hands grasps my balls, and her tongue does this thing no one's ever done to me before—it feels like it's wrapped along the underside of my base and rubbing up and down.

"I'm coming, Wren. Fuck! I'm coming!"

Ropes of cum decorate the tiled walls as I fall apart, accidentally ripping the shower head from the wall, sending water everywhere.

It doesn't faze me, seeing as once I turn the nozzle off, it'll take no time for my body to absorb the liquid.

But as my body relaxes, and my shower fantasy comes to a close, it hits me.

Wren seems interested in the possibility of us, and hopefully, dinner will be a step in the right direction.

If quick is what she's comfortable with, then so am I.

CHAPTER THIRTEEN

WREN

Alioth: Dinner at Agri'vi? If so, let me know what time you'd like me to pick you up.

Me: Fancy! And Dyv'i owned? Sounds great. I can be ready by 7PM. Is that too late?

Alioth: Not at all. See you then, darling.

What is it about that word that gets me so worked up? It blurs my vision as I try to concentrate on the times I have available for appointments tomorrow to get that hunk of a man in. I am way too excited to thread my hands through his dark curls.

Me: I'm booked solid all day tomorrow. Would you mind coming in after we close? Around 8PM??

My phone disappears from my hands, and I look up to find Fiona dangling it in my face as if she's trying to hypnotize me, a devilish smile on her face.

"Who are you texting?" she asks.

I yank it out of her grasp. "Alioth."

Fiona squeals. "The alien water daddy? Oh my God. What are you guys talking about? SHOW ME!"

"We're just planning dinner. Oh, and a haircut. We're trading services—swimming lessons for trims, I guess?"

"I can't wait to see him." She picks up a piece of paper from the check-in desk and fans herself. "Can I wash his hair?"

Laughter spills from my lips. "He won't be in until after you've left. I can try to sneak a picture while he's resting his head in the bowl."

"*Mhm*, if you're not riding his dick in the chair."

Clutching my imaginary pearls, I release a gasp. "Me? I'd never."

She gives me a look. "Right. Just like you'd never use a pool jet to get off. Get outta here and go to dinner. Give him head in the car while you're at it."

"Love ya, Fi! I'll let you know how it goes!"

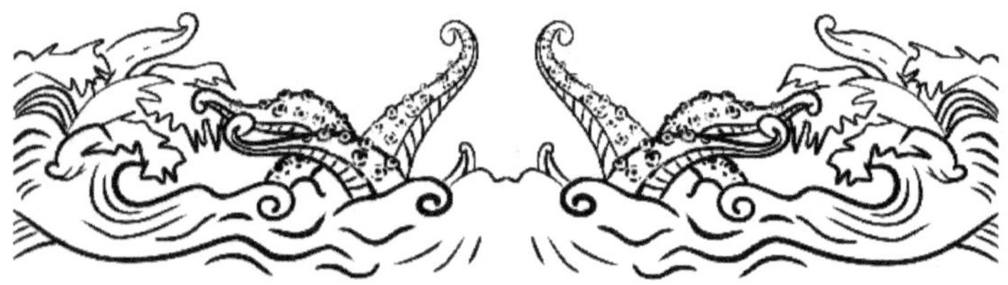

After an abnormally quiet car ride to the restaurant, I decide to start the actual conversation after we are seated and finished ordering our drinks and appetizer.

"Spiders. Kill or release?"

His eyes widen. "Release. How could you kill them? They're not doing anything."

I smack my hand down on the table, shaking the water in our tall glasses. "They're chasing me to try to bite my ass, Al! That's why they need to die!"

He cringes. "Please don't call me that," he quietly requests. "I much prefer Alioth."

Reaching for his hand, I give it a gentle squeeze. "I'm sorry. I'm a nickname bitch. I should've asked."

He turns my hand over and begins drawing designs in my palm with the tip of his pointer finger. "It's okay. I'm *not* a nickname bitch, and I *don't* kill spiders, even if they're coming for my ass."

My head tilts at his words. "Coming for your ass? I mean, you do have a nice ass, but I don't know about all that."

Alioth's chuckle is contagious—one of those that travels through every inch of your body to rid it of any negativity while adding a big smile to your face.

Damn, this man is fine, and I'd love nothing more than to be jumping into a relationship with him. I mean, come on... Hot alien, kind and thoughtful, selfless... Did I mention hot? I can't remember, because I'm too lost in his full-smile laugh, his tousled curls, fresh shave, tight dress shirt, and glasses. Yep. I'm a goner.

It's decided. When we get in that car, I'm totally reaching for his crotch.

I don't need years to figure out if someone's right for me. The chemistry is all there.

Dinner passes by in the blink of an eye, and before I know it, we're halfway back to my place, and holding hands.

"I want to hold something else," I blurt out, following it up with a slap from my other hand to shut me up. "I meant to only say that in my head."

He adjusts in his seat, steadily holding on to the wheel with his left hand. Then he pulls my hand into his lap. "Show me what you'd like to be holding, Wren."

Fuck, yeah. Word vomit for the win!

Scooching as far over in my seat as I can, I make quick work of his button and zipper, and sneak my hand under the waistband of his underwear.

His dick is hard but also soft, if that makes any sense at all. Pliable comes to mind. And the bead of pre-cum on the head is water-like—rather than sticky—as I smooth it down over the length of his cock for lubrication.

"That's better," I say.

Alioth slams his other hand to the wheel, startling me. "Fuck, Wren. Your hand feels so good wrapped around me. And your scent. It's—clouding my senses."

The car picks up speed after we turn onto my street.

CHAPTER FOURTEEN

ALIOTH

"I did use a new perfume," she comments.

Shaking my head, I focus on the road as best I can. "Your arousal. That's what I can smell." Five more driveways.

Her gasp has my cock twitching in her hand, and she releases a little moan.

"Pleased with yourself?" I ask her, whipping into the driveway and undoing my seatbelt at lightning speed.

When our eyes meet, she's nodding, her bottom lip between her teeth.

The silkiness of her skin against mine is tantalizing. So much so, I find my gaze scanning the street for any onlookers.

"You okay?" Wren asks.

I tilt my head toward the back. "Get in the backseat. There's more room, and it's tinted."

As she does, her glorious ass slides past my face, sending another strong whiff of her excitement straight to my nose, and I swear I go feral.

I'm not sure how it happens so fast, but before I know it, I'm in the backseat with my mouth on hers, plunging my tongue inside over and over to glide against hers.

Moans fill every inch of space around us as we consume each other. Then I lift her onto my lap and scooch my back against the seat, allowing her the chance to have full control of this.

But that's when I feel it...

My transformation... It's begun.

Play it cool, Alioth. You're an alien. She might not even notice in the heat of the moment.

I pull away, staring into her dark eyes while we both attempt to catch our breath.

She stares at me for a second, noticing the subtle differences that have begun, I'm sure. But instead of questioning me, she moves between my legs and onto her knees, leaning so her mouth hovers just over my dick.

As she looks down at it with heavy-lidded eyes, a trickle of spit falls from her mouth, landing directly on my tip. She collects it with her hand and slowly strokes me.

I lean my head back against the seat and close my eyes. "That feels really good, darling. Really fucking good."

"What about this?" she asks then sucks me into her mouth with gusto. Her expertise sends a bolt of electricity through me, lighting up every inch of my skin.

Reaching out for both of the car's grab handles, I resist placing either of my hands on the back of her head. I want her to enjoy this, too. I don't want to manhandle her.

Wren releases me with a pop and leans in to lick my bottom lip. "I need you to do me a favor, Alioth. Think you can do that?" I nod. "Thrust," she orders, then pulls me back into her mouth.

And thrust I do. Carefully, at first, unsure of how much she can take. But her moans and greedy hands want more, and I fucking deliver.

Fucking her delicious mouth, I near release, which has me tearing my hands away and wrapping her curls around my fist so I can plunge deeper and quicker.

"Right there, baby. Yes. Fuck. I'm going to come in your mouth."

Instead of retreating, she holds steady, preparing to swallow my load, and I explode. Stars cloud my vision, and I grunt my way through my release.

My mate just gave me the best head of my life. How the hell am I supposed to make her mine? Forever?

"You taste fucking good," Wren announces, yanking up her dress and placing one leg over each of my thighs to open herself to me. "And I hope your refractory time is just as."

I shoot her a wicked smirk before pulling her further up my lap, lining her slit up with my shaft and rubbing her up and down along it.

She pulls her dress off, revealing her lack of bra and pretty blue-laced briefs.

Not wasting a moment, I lean forward to lap at one of her hardened peaks while she runs one of her hands through my curls and pinches her free nipple with the other.

My transformation is now complete, and if she wants me to fuck her, I plan on showing her just how good at it I can be for her.

Only her.

CHAPTER FIFTEEN

WREN

Alioth is magnificent. With drenched-looking hair, scales along his temples, glowing aquamarine eyes and tattoos, and webbed hands, he makes water look delicious.

And I've never wanted to fuck someone more than I do right now.

"You're making a mess all over my cock, darling. How should we remedy that?"

I lean closer, brushing my mouth against his ear, and smile when I feel his body shiver. "I think you should push my underwear to the side and let me ride you."

"Or," he starts, grabbing both sides of the lacy material and ripping them right in half, "I could just do that."

All I can manage is a gasp as he drops both sides so they fall around where my thighs meet his and he grinds my bare pussy along his shaft until I can't handle it anymore.

Rising up higher on my knees, I plaster my mouth to his in a silent plea to hurry and get himself inside me. Thea has told me before that the Dyv'i are immune to sexually transmitted diseases and about how they are injected at a young age with something that has to be undone in their older age to even conceive, which is such a relief. I've never felt more relaxed about a hook-up before in my life. No worries about diseases? Or accidental pregnancies? Sign. Me. The. Hell. Up.

Alioth's hands squeeze my breasts, drift over my stomach, and down my thighs before retreating.

"If you're not inside me within the next minute, I'm going to lose my mind."

He offers me a wicked smirk. "We wouldn't want that now, would we? I need you fully present while I ravage you."

His gaze moves down as his hand wraps around his shaft. He pumps himself a few times before holding it steady for me.

I slowly lower, feeling his tip nudge at my opening, biting my lip in an effort to contain my moan.

Suddenly, two long navy tentacles covered in white suckers squeeze out from between his back and the seat. One of them snags both of my wrists and holds them above my head while the other moves to my mound, one sucker adhering to my clit and slowly pulsing over it.

"Fuck!" I yell. "That feels so good."

Alioth sits back and sets both of his hands on the seat, his gaze continuously sweeping me up and down. "You are absolutely exquisite. Now, show me, darling. Lower yourself on my cock and let me see how you'd like to ride me."

Ever so slowly, I sink down onto him, keeping my eyes locked on his. They glow brighter and brighter as each inch of him disappears inside me, and it takes every bit of restraint I possess to resist speeding up until I've taken all of him.

Once our pelvises finally meet, I shoot him a wink, and he releases a low growl.

One of his hands reaches out and wraps around my neck. He pulls me in and kisses me with such fervor, I pulse around him in response.

With his lips against mine, he briefly immobilizes me with three words. "Ride. Me. Darling." Then he releases me so he can sit back again and enjoy the view.

Lifting myself higher and higher until it feels like his tip might slip out, I slam myself back down and twist my hips in a circle.

Alioth grits his teeth as his head falls back against the headrest with closed eyes.

I pick up the pace, noticing how much I enjoy the slick cooling sensations of his member inside of me. It's unlike anything I've ever felt before, and I can definitely say that nothing will be able to compare.

"I'm not going to last long, Wren. How close are you?" he asks, a strain apparent both in his voice and on his face.

Thank God, because I've been close since before we started.

"So fucking close, Alioth. I want you to come with me. *Please*."

We begin to work in tandem, with him meeting my every thrust and hitting that special spot inside me as his suckers add more and more suction to my aching bud.

Our moans, whimpers, sighs, and grunts fill the car, our heaving breaths fogging up the already tinted windows, as we both get closer and closer to the finish line.

The tentacle bracing my arms above me slips down to my breasts, its suction cups latching on to my nipples as Alioth's hands softly cradle my face, guiding me to his mouth again.

With my hands now free, I run one of them through his curls, rubbing my other down his rigid pectorals and defined abs.

"Yes! Oh, Alioth. Right there. Don't stop!"

He spears his tongue into my mouth, groaning so loud, it vibrates my tongue.

I love his sounds; the way he shows me he's enjoying himself and can't get enough has me tipping off the very precipice of euphoria.

"I'm coming!" I scream.

As my walls clench around him, his hands push down on the tops of my thighs to keep himself inserted as far inside me as he can possibly be, where he continues small, tight thrusts.

"Uhh, fuck! Wren, yes, baby... I'm—fucking—coming!"

His cool, slippery cum splashes inside and flows down my walls, dripping out of me while Alioth remains inside, which is a bizarre feeling, to say the least.

But that's not all.

My orgasm... It's not letting up...

Closing my eyes, I slam my palms to his chest. "Uh, Alioth? *Mmm.*"

"What is it, darling?"

"I'm—*mhm*—still—*shit*—coming..."

CHAPTER SIXTEEN

ALIOTH

My mate twitches around my still-hard dick, her torso convulsing as she rides out the non-stop waves with her hands gripping the tops of my shoulders.

"I forgot to tell you, Wren. Our cum has a special property that extends the length of your pleasure. It's something we'll have to acclimate you to and work on. What do you need from me, baby? Talk to me."

I place a finger under her chin and draw her gaze to mine. Those dark-brown eyes are so heavy-lidded, it looks like she could fall asleep at any moment. And her cheeks? Rosy and flushed with passion.

"I need you"—she gasps—"to stay...inside me."

And then my beautiful blonde begins riding me again; much slower this time as the waves of her release begin to relax, but still.

Not wanting to miss a chance at more connection, and possibly orgasms, I move my thumb to her clit, circling at a steady pace.

My dress pants are soaked with both my cum and her wetness. It's the most glorious feeling.

Wren picks up her pace, using just the tip near her opening, where most human women possess the most nerve endings. Her noises alternate between gasps and little squeaks as she nears release again.

I pull her mouth to mine, whispering against her lips, "Come for me again. *Now*."

She erupts once more with a loud moan, her pace finally slowing and her body relaxing.

Finally, her body stills with my dick still inside her as she falls forward and cuddles into my chest.

"How the hell is your penis still this hard?"

My shoulders shake with quiet chuckles. "No refractory period. I could keep going, if you wanted me to."

"God, no. Not tonight. I'll die," she says.

I kiss her cheek and lift her up so my cock slips out of her and rests on my belly. Wren pulls her dress back on and sits beside me as I tuck myself back in and adjust my pants.

Turning toward her, I smile at the peaceful look on her face. "We should get you inside."

She shakes her head. "*We*? I can do it myself, thanks. Besides, you're probably super uncomfortable in those soaked pants and need to get home."

I pinch at the material covering my legs and let it go, proving a point. "Already dry, babe."

Her head tilts. "What? How?"

"I'm connected to water, remember? It takes nothing for me to absorb that stuff back into my body."

"Even mine?"

I nod. "Oh, yes. And it's divine. I could taste you during absorption."

She blushes and opens the door. "Listen… I think we can both agree that there's something between us. So, should we not play teenagers and make something of this?"

"Can you please be more clear?"

"Would you like to make things official, Alioth? I don't need a million dates to decide I'm interested in pursuing a relationship with you, so it's your call."

Can it really be this easy? It doesn't seem possible, let alone real. Maybe I'm dreaming… That has to be it. I've waited forty human years to find my person, and—

"Alioth?"

Refocusing my attention on her, I nod. "I'd love nothing more."

"Good." She smiles, my favorite front teeth pulling a return smile out of me. "So, I'll see you at your haircut tomorrow? *Boyfriend*?"

"Shit. I forgot… Raine had to take the day off for some appointments, so I'll be at the spa late. Can we actually reschedule for next week? We could do lessons and the haircut on the same day? *Girlfriend*?"

Wren exits the car, leaning only her head in through the crack. "For sure. I'll need this week off from you anyway to rest my vagina and tell my best friend, Thea, everything. So, rest your dick. Oh, and one last thing…"

I quirk a brow. "What's that?"

"Your penis seems very familiar, don't you think?"

My eye twitches as I cock my head to the side, mulling over my response. "What do you mean?"

She smirks. "Your dick and that fountain in your spa could be twins. Can I find out why someday?"

She waits a beat for my answer.

"You got it."

I scoot along the seat and give her a soft kiss before she retreats and walks up to her house. All the while, I watch from the driveway, still in disbelief over what just happened.

Wren knows what she wants, and lucky for me, I know what I want, too.

CHAPTER SEVENTEEN

WREN

Thea's brown curls sway as she spins in my salon chair. "What you do with hair has to be witchcraft."

I snicker. "How about schooling and years of experience?"

Unlike most high school students, I knew exactly what I wanted to do with my life. Playing with hair is something I've enjoyed since I was a child, so as soon as I graduated, off to cosmetology school I went. And I haven't looked back since. I've officially been in this profession for over ten years, and yeah, I'm fucking good at it.

"Sooooo, your hot alien boyfriend is coming in for a haircut tonight, huh?" Thea asks, waggling her brows up and down at a million miles a minute.

"He is." A blush creeps over my cheeks. "Do you think it's odd that we decided this so fast? Especially after sleeping together?"

She shrugs. "That's not up for me to decide. That's between the two of you. But do I think you're both completely capable of making a sound decision about that together?"

My gaze bounces between her eyes, unsure of her answer.

"Absolutely," she states.

I sigh with slight relief, her words bringing me hope.

And then Thea adds, "He has to know if he's your fated mate by now."

"But Kiran said not all subspecies are the same. It's not like I've purchased a plant from him like you did. How would I even know?"

Her brows furrow, and she stops the chair with her shoe. "How do you feel about him, Wrenny?"

I sit with her question, paying close attention to how my chest warms and expands with the thought of our connection. "Like he could be the one."

"Even though I denied it and fought it time and time again, that's the feeling I had with Kiran. I just didn't know it, nor did I want to admit it. Don't get your hopes up, but don't close that door yet, either. You've always been way more passionate and open to love than I've ever been."

"You remember what my mom always says—our hearts are doors. Whether you keep it open, shut, or locked, there's still a possibility for someone to enter. But when you remove the door completely because you gave up, you doom yourself to a lonely life." Spinning her to face me, I bend down and embrace her. "I'm so glad you found love, Thea. There's no one more deserving of their fated mate having the key to your heart than you."

Thea pushes me away. "Ugh, yuck. Love you and all, but you know how I feel about hugs." She rolls her eyes with a wide grin on her face. "But thank you. I feel like Kiran makes me nicer."

We burst out in laughter, because truer words have never been spoken. Then the door dings.

And in walks both of our hot alien hunks...

The power sweeping the room matches the colors clouding our senses—sage-green and ocean-blue skin to match the Earth, where they've come to find their fated mates. Oh, how I hope I'm Alioth's mate.

"Hey, sweet girl," Kiran greets Thea, kissing her on the cheek. "And hi to you, too, Wrenny. Good to see you." He gives me a quick hug before moving aside.

"Hi, darling," Alioth says, granting me a kiss on the forehead.

Damn. These pet names are enough to do me in. Thea is just as captivated as I am; it's clear as day on her face. Best friends, with alien males that know how to rock our sexual worlds? We couldn't have manifested better for ourselves if we tried.

Kiran quirks a brow and shoots a smirk my way. "Wren, I finally got to meet your man outside. He seems like a nice guy."

My eyes dance between the three of them. "Puh-lease, like you'd say anything mean with the guy standing right here. You're too nice, Kiran. Alioth is a grumpy old man."

"*Oooo!*" Thea chuckles. "With that look, we should get out of here. They'll be lucky if they make it through a haircut." She pushes Kiran toward the door, yelling, "Nice to meet you, Alioth. We'll talk more soon!" over her shoulder.

"What look?" I ask, tilting my head in her direction.

"This one," Alioth adds, staring at me with glowing, molten eyes that nearly melt the clothes from my body.

I nod. "*Oh.* That one. Yeah, you guys might want to get outta here. There's a very big chance I might have sex in the salon tonight."

CHAPTER EIGHTEEN

ALIOTH

As I watch Kiran and his mate leave, I find myself wondering why more of us Dyv'i don't interact and get to know our various subspecies better. I'd like to learn more about the Cēd'oh, and in turn, teach him some things about my Wa'gōah culture.

It's obvious how close Thea and Wren are—similar to a sibling relationship, it seems. Maybe the four of us can spend some time together soon. That way, I can chat with Kiran about how to reveal the truth to Wren about our mated tie.

Once Wren shuts and locks the doors and presses a button that has blinds extending down from the edge of the ceiling to cover the windows, she spins toward me with a flirty smile. "Now, listen to me. Let's make it through this haircut, and then you can fuck me ten different ways on every surface of this place. Got it?"

With a slow nod, I step closer, making her catch her breath and emit that delicious arousal I love so much. "Shall we make this a game, my darling?"

Her throat bobs with a swallow. "What kind of game?"

"Give me a nice haircut while I touch you as you work, and I'll fuck you on any surface of your choosing in here. Mess up, and you'll be forced to watch me get myself off in that chair of yours."

One of her eyebrows rises. "And if I have a hard time choosing which of those I'm into?"

I shrug. "You're telling me you're willing to wait for my cock to be inside you?"

A loud sigh escapes her. "Let's just see how this goes, okay? Get your ass in the damn seat."

The chair squeaks as I plop into it, and I make a mental note to give it some WD-40, as well as check around the salon for anything else that needs to be fixed or updated.

Wren gets to work, spraying my hair, twirling around me, and spinning the chair like we're in some type of dance, combing, cutting, and clipping my hair as she concentrates with the cutest little face—tongue out and all.

And now, I refuse to keep my hands to myself any longer. We're to the good part of cutting the longer, curlier top portion, and I'm fucking determined to have her make a mistake. The thought of her watching me work myself over has my cock hard as steel already.

I brush my fingers down both sides of her hips until I meet the edge of her skirt then slip it up, showcasing another pair of lace briefs, thighs with the most beautiful dimples, and hips that desire to be held.

I leave her skirt bunched and run one of my fingers over the section of her panties covering her slit, gathering some of her wetness that has escaped through the delicate material.

"You're dripping wet for me, baby," I whisper, licking her essence from my digit as I focus on her face.

With her eyes glued to my mouth, she gasps, crossing one leg over the other as she takes a quick breath before moving her concentration to her own hands and cutting another piece of my hair.

Wren clears her throat, continuing her cuts in silence as my hands continue to run over her hips and mound.

"Do the arms of this chair fold down or anything?"

She smirks. "They do. I wanted size-inclusive chairs for my salon, because everyone deserves to feel beautiful when they walk in here, no matter what. Here, hold these."

Holding the scissors and comb in my hand for her, I reflect on what she just said as she unlatches the arms and leaves them to dangle below the seat. My mate is a truly amazing human being; thinking of others and trying to change the world with her positivity and inclusivity. The world needs way more people like her.

Once she stations herself back in front of me, I shove the tools back at her and sweep her up onto my lap, her legs spread so that her cunt lines up directly with my hard cock.

She gasps, grasping my shirt with her free hand, which has me chuckling.

A blush works its way up her cheeks. "How am I supposed to finish from here?"

"You'll find a way." I start rolling my hips to give her some friction. "But first, feel how hard you make me, darling. I hope you're almost done."

CHAPTER NINETEEN

WREN

I'm just about to make my last cut when Alioth yanks me from his lap and sets me back on my feet, which, in turn, messes up the last snip. Asshole!

He can tell by the look on my face what happened, and I have a feeling he did it on purpose.

I think my hot alien hunk wants me to watch him get off. And I guess, in a way, he's spot-fucking-on, because that is *exactly* what I want. There is something about watching a man pleasuring himself. *Damn it*, I swear there's some wetness dripping down my leg at the mere thought of him doing that.

Alioth *tsks*. "Looks like there's been a mistake with my haircut, ma'am."

Skirt still bunched, I put a hand to my hip. "Oh no. Whatever shall we do?" I can tell by his quirked brows that he might not fully understand the sarcasm leaking from my words, and that's fine. Actually, it's quite hilarious, because he probably thinks this is going to upset me.

Well, *Mr. Water Daddy*, I think you've met your match...

"Panties off, sit on the floor, and spread your legs," he orders in that signature grumpy tone, his eyes glowing bright as he unzips his pants and frees his hard dick.

Grabbing a towel from behind the check-in desk, I plop myself on the ground before him and can't help but lick my lips in response to the view. I mean, who could? A tall, broad, blue-skinned alien male with curly, deep-navy locks, ripple tattoos, and a large hand wrapped around his cock and ready to play? *Mhm*. Lady porn right here.

As he loosely pumps his hand up and down his shaft, his eyes dart down to my center. "*Fuck*. I love your light dusting of hair and how it showcases your glistening arousal for me. Makes me want to lap up every. Fucking. Drop."

My head falls back. "*Mmm*. Can I please touch myself now?"

"No." A growl rumbles from his chest; one that crawls right under my skin and rolls over my nerves.

With hooded eyes and a wicked smirk, I reach down to my core, collect some of my wetness, and plunge my fingers into my mouth, sucking them clean. Alioth strokes faster and harder, while his eyes glow even brighter, and the muscle in his jaw ticks.

"Do it again," he orders.

I shake my head. "You said not to. I should follow the rules."

Suddenly, his two tentacles unleash from behind him and dart toward me, grabbing one of my hands and placing it to my opening.

"Do. It. Again," he repeats, growling at the end of each syllable. "I'm close."

That piques my interest, so I keep my hand where it is until the tentacle decides to release me. Then I pop more of my arousal between my lips, moaning around my fingers as I suck it all off.

Rising to my feet, I walk over to him and kiss him, moaning into his mouth. "Can you taste me?"

He nods, grunting with pumps that extend up over his tip and bottom out where the base of his shaft meets his balls. His hips rock up and down as much as they can in the salon chair.

Moving my lips to his ear, I whisper, "I need you to come for me, baby. *Please*. Let me watch."

"Uh, *fuck*, Wren!"

I quickly step behind him and run my hands down over his chest as his orgasm sweeps through him. Thick ropes of clear cum spurt out from the head of his penis, spilling onto his shirt and splashing the tips of my fingers.

I immediately plunge my fingers into my mouth yet again, swirl my tongue around to collect everything, pull his head to the side, and glue my lips to his once more. We moan into one another, our tongues exploring each other's mouths before we break apart again.

As his breathing levels back out, I remain wrapped around him, peppering his cheek with kisses. "That was hot," I whisper into his ear.

"It was even hotter tasting myself on your tongue," he replies. "Now, get over here and sit on my cock."

CHAPTER TWENTY

ALIOTH

The moment Wren steps before me, I have my hands and tentacles wrapped around her in various places on her body and am tugging her up so that her knees are on my shoulders, the tops of her feet are cradled in the hands, and my tentacles are holding her torso up.

Wren lets out a little squeal, and I wish I could take the time to tell her what I have planned, but I'm rather distracted.

Her gorgeous cunt is level with my mouth, and I can't help but breathe her in as I rub my nose against the soft dusting of hair covering her mound.

"What the hell are you doing?" she demands.

I place a kiss on both of her inner thighs before gazing up at her. "There's no way I'm fucking you until I've had my dessert."

We sway a little in the chair, and Wren yelps again. "We are going to fall."

"No, we're not. I've got you."

"Alioth…"

Flattening my tongue against her clit, I hum, hoping to distract her. "At least if you fall here, there's no drowning."

She bucks against my face before leaning those perfect hips back. "Don't be an ass, ya grump."

Does she really think name calling is going to bother me at this moment in time? Especially as she moves her hips further up and plants herself on my face?

"Oh no. Are you trying to suffocate me with your perfect pussy, darling?"

I'm pretty sure the whole world can sense her eye roll. "You're incorrigible. What do I have to do for you to let me down from here?"

Ah. The question I thought she'd never ask.

"It's easy. Fuck my face to orgasm, and then you can ride my cock until we both come together. Deal?"

An uneasy groan travels past her lips, and for a brief moment, I consider letting her have her way, but I'm much too stubborn for that. I won't let her fall. Well, not literally. But metaphorically? Oh, yes. She'll be falling. Off the precipice, into euphoria, and all on my fucking tongue.

"I want it, Wren."

She gasps at my words. "Want what? Exactly?" Her questions come out breathy.

"You. Riding my face. Now. Please."

"Since you said please…"

Moving her hips up toward my face, I dart out my tongue, quickly finding her clit, and flicking up and down. Wren moans above me, gyrating her hips in search of more pressure.

Little does she know there are some alterations my body makes just for her that I haven't used yet…

Yes, the scales are present, the tentacles are, too, but I think it's time for more.

My tongue grows colder.

"Fuck, Alioth. That feels so good. Does your tongue turn to ice or something?"

I place a swift kiss to her core before briefly pulling away. "Let's just say that my tongue is capable of temperature play."

"Nice. Yeah. Okay. I need it back, please."

As I give her what she wants, her hips rock faster and faster as she nears completion.

So, I stretch my tongue, still keeping some of it connected to her swollen bud, while the tip grows longer, seeking out her opening.

It dives in, leaking warm water, and I discover a whole new version of Wren.

"Oh. My. God," she stammers. Her hips do this amazing thing where she bobs up and down on my tongue but still manages this forward slant at the end as a way to gain friction against her sweet bundle of pleasure.

"Alioth. Fuck—Me—Whatever you're doing, don't stop. Yes. Right there!"

I'm literally about to combust. She needs to come so that I can impale her with my shaft and bring us to one last orgasm together.

Almost before the thought has finished crossing my mind, she catapults off the edge, drenching me completely with her cum and the water I was injecting her with.

I slowly retreat from inside and against her, carefully lowering her and letting her limbs go, allowing her to rest against my *very* hard cock. "That was fucking hot, Wren."

CHAPTER TWENTY-ONE

WREN

The spa bell rings as I enter, announcing my arrival to whoever may be inside.

A little girl with adorable braids pops out from behind the computer, standing on the desk and wiping off the check-in counter. I can't help but cringe as I watch the dribbling penis fountain she's getting dangerously close to with the rag. Oh no...

I race over to the ledge and remove the fountain, taking a few steps back.

"Thanks!" she says. "Mommy always moves the fountains for me."

A chuckle bursts out of me. Thank God for kids and their innocence. And on second thought, I really need to have a conversation with Alioth about having this in his spa when there's an actual child that seems to frequent the place!

"Del, how are you doing?" Raine shouts, rounding the corner. When she catches sight of me, she smiles. Her braids stretch down well past her shoulders, bright red wrapped within the strands to create beautiful dimensions. "Hey, Wren. How are you?"

I smile back at her. "I'm good. Just watching this little one clean."

Raine comes up behind the girl and lifts her onto the floor with a *hmph*. "This here is my daughter, Delilah. She likes to come to work with me sometimes, which I don't mind, because then I get to put her to work."

"I can see that. You do great work, Delilah!"

Delilah trots over to me and looks up into my face. "Thank you, Miss... What's your name?" She holds out her small hand to me.

"Wren. It's lovely to meet you, Delilah."

We shake hands. "Same to you! Mommy calls me Del. You can, too, if you want," she sing-songs. It's fucking adorable.

But Raine breaks our greeting with a yell. "Delilah! What happened to the last fountain? You're not supposed to touch any of the ones up high."

"I grabbed it, actually," I tell her, holding it up in the air with both hands. "Was trying to get it out of her way."

"Yep! Miss Wren helped me out, Mommy. Doesn't it look so nice now?"

Her mom gives me a grateful grin, moving toward me with quick steps. "Thank you for moving Freddie," she whispers. "I try to get it out of the way ahead of time whenever she comes in, because...well, you know, but she beat me to the desk before I could get them all. I was literally just coming back for it."

My voice lowers to match her whispers. "I'm sorry, *Freddie*?" I laugh. The penis fountain has a name?

She places her hands on her hips. "When you spend the last five years with that thing stuck in your line of vision, you start to feel like it needs to be named. Shit. Half of my shifts, Freddie is the only thing I can talk to. It's absurd."

"I'd have to agree, and I get it," I reply, unable to break my smile.

Water begins trickling on my hand, and it's then that I realize I've somehow tipped Freddie, spilling water onto the floor.

"Oh, shit!" I yell, a little too loudly for a kid being in the room. "Oops, sorry!"

I try to right the fountain and myself, but wind up slipping on the puddle I've created instead, falling right back onto my ass. Thankfully, I manage to keep Fred—the fountain, I mean—safe.

"What the hell are you doing?"

Alioth.

Opening my eyes, I scan the room until my eyes lock with his, and I offer him an awkward grin. "Um..."

Raine's daughter squeals with excitement at the sight of the tall blue alien, breaking out into a run right for him with outstretched arms. "Miss Wren slipped and fell on her booty, Mr. A!"

He chuckles, and its warmth settles deep down in my chest. Seems to me, the grumpy alien spa owner has a soft spot for kids. He crouches down and extends his arms to the little girl, wrapping them around her as soon as she flings herself at him.

What is it about men playing with kids? *Ugh.* The sight has my ovaries literally screaming!

Alioth peppers her cheek with kisses, making her giggle, before placing her back on the ground. "Want to go swim in one of the pods? I guess I can give your mom a break to come play with you."

She spins around with her eyes and mouth open as wide as they can go before asking, "Can we, Mommy? Pleaseeeeeeee."

With a restful sigh, Raine holds out her hand to Delilah and nods, and they scurry toward the hallway. Raine pauses to look at my partner over her shoulder. "You're too soft, old man. And why don't you try using that friendliness with me, too? Or should I give Del my job?"

He grunts and rolls his eyes in response before holding a hand out to me and helping me up.

"I'm okay," I assure him, fighting back a smile at the one piece of hair I cut too short he's tried hiding in his luscious curls.

No one else would notice but me. Well—or other cosmetologists.

His gaze runs ups and down my body as he checks me over. "Well, that's good. And Freddie?"

I push the fountain into his arms, sending more water flying around us. "Even you call the fountain that?"

"It's like code or something. Customers already look at it funny. Sometimes, Raine and I can joke around about him with no one else knowing."

I shake my head. "You two are something else..."

"Trust me, we know." Alioth leans down to place a kiss on the top of my head. "Are you ready for your final swim lesson tomorrow?"

"Very ready." I smile widely, beaming with both excitement and pride. This is the first time I've been able to stick to swimming lessons and face my fear of water in my entire life. I guess what they say is true; you're never too old to learn something new.

"Good, but... Could you come to my house earlier for dinner? There's something I'd really like to discuss with you."

"Is this something *bad*?" I ask, because there's nothing worse than being told a conversation needs to happen but basically being told you have to wait until they're ready to tell you.

His dark curls sway with the shake of his head. "No. At least, I don't think so. It's a good thing. Plus, Freddie will be there."

Giving him a playful shrug, I bat my lashes at him. "Fine. I'll promise to meet early for this *something* dinner, but only if you agree to finally tell me what your connection is to that fountain while I'm there."

Alioth's throat bobs with a hard swallow. "Deal."

CHAPTER TWENTY-TWO

ALIOTH

It's nearly impossible to keep my eyes off of my blonde beauty. Even though we're set for her last swimming lessons—she's perfected the doggy paddle, getting minorly splashed in the face, and floating on her back—Wren worked really hard to make herself irresistible today.

Relaxed curls that stretch past her shoulders, a smoky eye, and glossy nude lips. I can't help but stare into her gorgeous brown eyes, wish to run my fingers through her hair, and desire to glue my mouth to hers.

Even my penis agrees, if the tightness in the crotch of my pants is anything to go by.

I didn't dress up nearly as much as Wren. To her leather pants and low-cut V-top, I have khakis and a polo. Yes, like a golfer. I guess I'm channeling my inner-dad? Is that what happens when hitting my age? Sandals. Polos. Khakis. Belts.

What's next? A visor?

I only know about those damn things because of a past customer who used to visit the spa. And Raine, who has taught me a lot of lingo and things while working for me.

"Alioth?"

Startled, I blink. "Hm? Sorry. What were you saying?"

Wren smirks. "Have you been checking me out this entire time?"

Folding my hands and setting my elbows atop the table to prop my chin up, I shoot her what I hope is a panty-melting smirk. "Guilty."

She nods, forking the last piece of potato on her plate. "Well, how would you feel if I unbuttoned my pants right now?"

My body twitches of its own accord, like it wants to move closer to her without my say-so.

But Wren holds up her hand. "Hold up, old man. Not like that. I ate too much, and I can't breathe."

Laughter bursts from somewhere deep in my chest. Smiling and laughing like this hasn't always come easy to me. I've always been sort of a grump. But with my mate? She shines through the darkest haze, and all those happy things I never used to do? Well, I do them now.

And the best part?

I like it. Love it, actually.

Suddenly, Wren is crawling into my lap, hooking my arms around herself. "You're doing it again."

"Sorry. I—I can't help it, okay? You're stunning, and I want nothing more than to fuck you seven ways to Sunday on this dinner table."

She gasps, rubbing a hand down my chest. "What if I want you to fuck me in the pool, though?"

My dick immediately stiffens, like it's gearing up for a sword fight. *No, no. We want this, you stupid thing. Be patient.*

"You okay?"

Opening my eyes, I decide to somewhat tell the truth. "Sorry. Got distracted again. My dick is trying to fight."

Her hand claps over her mouth to stifle a chuckle. "Fight? Who? Me?"

"Well, not fight in a bad way. More like, fight out of my pants to reach you."

She nods a few times, leaning in close. "I think you need to tell me what I came early for, and why Freddie is present, because if I don't have you inside of me within the next fifteen minutes, I might just take Freddie for a spin."

"You'd ride a fountain? Made of stone?"

Wren shrugs. "I'm sure weirder things have been inserted inside holes."

I roll my eyes and fall back with laughter. "You're going to be the death of me."

"Well, till death do us part, they say... Righ—" The words die on her tongue as she stares at me in shock. Obviously, that was supposed to be an inside thought.

Her hand darts out to pinch my lips closed. "Don't say anything. I didn't mean to say that. I'm so—"

I wrap my hand around her wrist, prompting her to free my lips, and playfully bite down on her pointer finger, drawing a squeal from her.

"Actually, I'm glad you brought that up... Because..." Fuck. How do I say this? How did Kiran break the news to Thea? What is the right way? *Fuck it.* "You're my mate."

Beats of silence pass between us where both of our eyes dart from one eye to the other, each of us waiting for someone to say whatever the hell is supposed to come next.

And then... Freddie gushes out water like a geyser, drenching both us and the table.

CHAPTER TWENTY-THREE

WREN

I squeal as Alioth abruptly stands from the chair and carries me away from the fountain-created rainstorm before he sets me on my feet outside of the splash zone and stomps back toward the table.

"Damn it, Freddie! If you can understand me, this needs to stop!" he yells. "I told her. Now, stop the stream. It's embarrassing."

Freddie—it's hilarious that Alioth has also taken on calling him by the name—stops gushing, and when Alioth heaves a sigh of relief, the fountain gives one last short burst that hits Alioth's face before finally resuming its usual flow.

As Alioth turns to face me, with droplets of water trickling down his face, I can't help the laughter that spills from my lips.

But the bright glow of his eyes and the beginning formations of the scales on the sides of his face quiet me.

This is my mate. *Alioth*. An alien. He's the one I'm destined to be with for the rest of my life, and all it took was a crazy spa visit to find him.

"So... Are you *really* my mate?" Can't be too sure.

He nods, slowly moving closer.

I cross my arms. "How do you know?"

One of his long, slender fingers points behind him. "That stupid fucking fountain that is twins with my dick. My subspecies—us Wa'gōah—we are all gifted one upon reaching our age of adolescence, told that it will finally flow with never-ending waters the moment we find our fated mate. That thing sat collecting dust all this time, until—"

I gasp. "Until I came in. That's why it burst out of nowhere and drenched us." My hands find their way to my mouth, covering my shock. "You knew this whole time!"

Alioth nods again. "I just didn't know how to tell you. And when you told me about Thea and Kiran, I was so worried about how much you knew of the Dyv'i. Every subspecies usually sticks to themselves, so we don't necessarily know about each other's mate customs, and I hoped you all wouldn't put two-and-two together regarding the fountain incident. But I also wasn't sure what Thea might've shared with you regarding our true forms. We vow to only tell our mates, hoping not to scare humans off, since we have figured out so many of us are destined for your kind, but I know how deeply friendships can run. I wouldn't be surprised if Thea shared that truth with you."

"Thea and I are practically sisters, but while she told me about the penis plant that brought her and Kiran together, she told me nothing about the transformation part. Now that you mention it, though, I'm totally causing a fight over this. I wanna know how good the sex is, with the actual details!"

He tilts his head at me. "You *want* to know?"

I raise my brows. "Uh, *yeah*. Girl talk, don't ya know?"

His shoulders rise with a deep breath as his gaze rakes over me. "I guess I do now..."

Beats of silence pass between us as he moves even closer, taking my hands in his.

"Babies."

He quirks a brow, and his head tilts. "What about them?"

"Thea has never wanted kids, but me? I want lots of them. And I want to be the crazy mom who blasts screamer rock in the drop-off line."

Alioth nods. "Kids sound great. I can have my injection reversed whenever you're ready to start trying."

Taking quick glances around his house, I think of other stipulations that are important to mention. "I want to move in here, and I want to keep working at the salon. Oh, and I want a dog. Childhood dogs are the best, and kids should grow up with one."

"You can move in whenever you're ready. I'd never want you to stop working unless you want to. And a dog sounds great. I've never owned one, but sure."

I smile up at him. "Is there nothing I can say that will make you change your mind?"

His brows furrow. "Do you want me to change my mind?"

"No." I shake my head. "I'm just making sure."

"The only way this wouldn't work is if you rejected the mating bond. So, really, it's not me you have to worry about. It could be the other way around."

Leading him back to the table, I push him down in the chair as I remain standing before him. "Give me your worst."

And then I begin to undress, utterly obsessed with the way his eyes continue to glow and his body progresses in its transformation.

As his eyes repeatedly rake over me from head to toe, he almost whispers his list to me. "I like my facial hair and my hair in shaggy curls. I'm a stickler about the lawn and like it cut a certain way. I'm shit at laundry and never separate colors like it seems many humans do. Um... Oh, and I only do grocery pick-ups, because going inside the store pisses me off, and I'm always on the verge of running someone's granny over with my cart."

My head bobs along to the list. "Doesn't sound like you're terrible to live with, seeing as I love your facial hair and curly mop, I hate cutting the lawn, laundry isn't a big deal, and if I can stop worrying about fighting off any feral old ladies with my cart in the freezer section, I'm golden. So, it looks like we might be good to go. But I must say, this doesn't mean you'll never find me annoying. There could come a day when I do or say something that causes a fight."

Alioth rises so we're almost skin to skin, removing his shirt and pants to stand in just his swim trunks. And damn... There's no way I could ever forget how fucking fine this man is.

With one finger, he tilts my face up so our eyes meet. "I'd rather spend a lifetime fighting with you than spend even a *day* without your love, darling." His Wa'gōahn accent lilts along with the pet name perfectly.

I sigh. Could he get any dreamier?

"Let's get this last lesson over with," I say, dragging him behind me toward the pool. "The sooner it's done, the sooner we can fuck, and I really need that, okay?"

"Noted," his gruff voice replies.

CHAPTER TWENTY-FOUR

ALIOTH

Today is the day Wren is going to try to go underwater. We're talking fully submerged, head and all.

It's going to be hard for her, that I do know, but I just need her to try. And not just once; at least twice.

Side by side, we enter the pool holding hands, the truth of our bond taking up space around us.

"How are you feeling? Need an orgasm before all this?"

She chuckles. "Do you think it's weird to have honest conversations like this? Is it weird to you to outright ask someone something like that?"

I mull over the question for a moment. "I mean... I don't think so. Sexuality shouldn't be something to be ashamed of. And besides, shouldn't we be able to talk about anything seeing as we're mates who are sexually active with one another?"

A smile so wide it's easy to spot in my periphery lights up her whole face. "And this is how I know we are definitely meant to be. I feel like I can completely be myself with you—crazy topics and questions and all."

We reach the ground of the pool's shallow end before I pull her to me, smoothing the flyaways back from her face. "I love your crazy questions and surprising discussion topics. You prove to me all the time that it's okay to be completely authentic because there's someone out there who wants to find the person they *can* talk that way with. Not everyone finds that."

"I'm glad to see it's rubbed off on you. And to answer your question, I wouldn't mind a pre-possible-drowning orgasm." The corner of her mouth pulls up in this sexy smirk as her eyelids slightly drop.

I walk her backward to the side of the pool, pushing her up against the wall and using my feet to push hers closer together. "Any requests, my darling?"

Wren nods, licking her lips as she stares at my mouth. "Confession."

"Go for it."

"I've always wondered what it'd be like to be thoroughly fucked by one of your tentacles," she states with a casual shrug.

Laughter spills from my mouth. "Is my cock not enough for you, my mate?" I ask, boxing her in between my arms and rubbing the tip of my nose up the shell of her ear.

She sighs, lightly running her hands up my arms. "Oh," she breathes, "it is, but when a male like yourself has these extra...members...I feel the need to take them for a spin."

Suddenly wondering if I can use this to our lesson's advantage, I decide to take her up on the offer. Ever so slowly, I unfurl my tentacles from behind me as my transformation continues, grasping both sides of her bottoms and gently pulling them off. The fabric floats to the surface, and I make quick work of tossing them up onto the ledge.

Before I make another move, Wren is stretching up on her tiptoes and licking up the length of my neck, sending chills down my spine.

"How do you make water taste so good, Alioth?" she breathes against my mouth, and I close my eyes to gain some composure. I have no control around this woman.

I give her lip a quick nip, which pulls a high-pitched squeal from her. "Be careful, darling, or I might have to cut the foreplay short."

As she settles between my arms with her shoulders against the stone ledge, she devours me with her eyes, pulling her lip between her teeth. "I assure you, foreplay isn't needed," she tells me. "I've been ready since your transformation finished."

I take her chin between my thumb and forefinger, holding her gaze on mine. "Keep those eyes on me while I enter you, baby. I want to see how you react to my tentacles slipping deep inside."

Using one of my tentacles to pull one of Wren's legs to the side and spread her open before me, I slowly wind the other tentacle up her other leg, softly caressing her slit before plunging into her tight heat.

"Oh," Wren moans, barely able to keep her eyes open. "That—"

With my mouth against hers, I finish for her. " —feels fucking amazing, I know."

My lips connect with hers, and we absorb each other's noises as I continue fucking her with my tentacle. And before I can register her next move, Wren's hand is inside my trunks and pumping my dick with rushed abandon.

Everything is muddling my brain.

Wren. She's my mate. And she knows.

And our sex is unlike anything I've ever experienced, or would ever be able to put into words.

I can't help but feel proud that she can still find pleasure here with me, despite the fact I'm connected to something that brings her so much fear.

So, in between kisses, I use one hand to pick her up and wrap her legs around my waist while the other pinches her nose closed. My mouth will be able to provide her with air while we take a quick plunge beneath the surface.

I pick up the pace with my tentacle, feeling her edging toward release, and drag her down until we're both completely covered in water.

But with a jab to my throat and a painful twist to my cock, she breaks free of my grasp and rises above the surface.

"Get the hell off of me!" she screams, racing toward the stairs.

Oh, hell...

This was a mistake.

CHAPTER TWENTY-FIVE

WREN

Who the hell does he think he is? Impaling me with his stupid tentacle and nearly drowning me while in the throes of passion...

Absolutely not.

As I emerge from the pool, gasping for breath from both the fear of being pulled underneath the surface and boiling fury, Alioth is on my heels.

His hand just barely grabs my arm, and I whip around to face him, jabbing my finger up toward his face.

"Why the hell would you do that, Alioth? You didn't even ask me! Not even a warning, either, other than grabbing my fucking nose a millisecond before you pulled me under."

He releases me, regret blanketing his expression. "I'm so sorry. I wasn't thinking. I—I just thought that taking the pressure off would help."

"No!" I shout, moving so we are chest to chest. "You thought using my own fantasy against me would *what*? Erase my fears? News flash, Mr. *Mate*, I might *never* get over this fear, and *you* would have to live with that."

Alioth holds up his hands in surrender. "I never said you had to. Nor did I ever say that your fear would be a limit hard enough for me to want to push you away. Don't you understand, Wren? Fated mates strive to be together, no matter what. I'm sorry, darling. I really am."

My eyes burn as his apology sinks in, and I can't keep the tears at bay.

"That really scared me," I murmur, finally allowing myself to feel all the emotions my anger was trying to protect me from. "And I don't want to do it again."

"Baby," he coos, hugging me against his chest. "I would never make you do anything you don't want to. Never again, you hear me? Unless you ask me to. Come here."

He leads me to a chair and pulls me into his lap while stroking my hair, and his peppering kisses send my mind wandering in a thousand different directions.

I snuggle in deeper, breathing in his ocean-breeze scent, wondering what something like this could do to us. How can I expect him to accept someone utterly afraid of something he loves?

"I don't know what kind of galactic forces pushed us together, but are you *really* sure you can live with that? I need you to be confident in your decision, Alioth. I don't want to be loved halfway."

Easing me off of his chest, he picks me up with ease, setting me back down so that I'm straddling him. We are eye-to-eye now, and he has my rapt attention, even with the blurriness in my vision.

"I accept every version of you that has, does, or will exist, my mate—the likes and dislikes, the fears, and everything in between.

Love is adaptive." He places a chaste kiss to the tip of my nose. "I'm so proud of the strides you've already made with your fear of the water, but, baby, even if that's all the progress you make, and that's all you ever do with it, that's still enough. And besides, it doesn't need to be enough for me, it only matters this much to you. But I do have a request."

I groan. "Oh, God... What?"

He makes a clicking sound with his tongue. "Our kids will need to learn how to swim, because I'll be damned if they drown."

A smile overtakes my face. "And they'll have the best teacher on the planet. No, wait, in the universe. Absolutely, teach them to swim, and I'll try my best to be brave around them when it comes to the water..."

"You're already brave. Plus, I can always remind you how good water can be when it comes to some shower sex where the water *doesn't* hit your face." He winks.

Judging by the bulge reforming between us, the visual must be a good one for him to already be growing hard again.

That's when I realize I never put my bottoms back on. "Oh my!" I yelp.

"What?"

Glancing between where my suddenly warm core and his covered hard-on meet and his eyes, I scrunch up my face at him. "We're trying to have a serious conversation, but you failed to tell me I'm still partially naked."

His lips part to reveal his gorgeous smile. "That was the whole point. Doesn't communication like this sometimes lead to the next base?"

"Ya know, for being a grumpy old man who's been waiting his whole life to find his mate, you're good at this. Have you been reading romance books?"

"No." He shakes his head, and a few droplets of water from his curls rain down on my chest. "Why?"

I rub the water in before reaching inside his trunks to grasp his dick in my hand. "Because something like this surely should've pushed us apart in one of those third act breakups. Miscommunication has a way of doing that. But, here we are, about to have the best kind of sex."

He tilts his head in this adorable alien way that tells me he has never heard of it. "Hand jobs?"

My chest moves with a silent chuckle. "Oh my God, no. Makeup sex."

All at once, scales ripple down his face and his tentacles move out to each side from his back. In his true form, he's a sight to behold, and I'm so fucking lucky to be the only one who gets to enjoy him like this.

"Tentacle fucking again?" he questions.

I shake my head in response, wondering if our bond is strong enough for him to know exactly what I need.

His tentacles latch on to my hips and lift me slightly so he can free his member and line it up with my opening before the tentacles slowly lower me over him, inch by inch, until he's fully sheathed inside my wet heat. Moans fall from both of our lips when he's buried to the hilt and we're just staring into each other's eyes, breathing heavily.

"Good, because while that's hot and all, nothing quite compares to the way your cunt grips my cock. Now, do you want to move? Or shall I use my tentacles to continue what we started?"

Leaning in close, I whisper against his lips, "Tentacles. And no touching until we come. Let's just watch each other come undone. Deal?"

Alioth doesn't answer. Instead, he takes my hands and places them under my suit top before lifting his arms to grab the top of the chair.

If a show is what he wants, a show is what he'll get...

CHAPTER TWENTY-SIX

ALIOTH

Fuck, fuck, fuck.

My mate is a sight to behold as she is lifted and lowered on my cock while playing with her nipples. She pinches and twists them, her perfect mouth shaped in an O as she rides the waves leading straight to euphoria.

And before I can register what's happening, my balls draw up, and an orgasm racks my body.

"Damn it. Yes, baby! Yes!" The words spill from my mouth.

Wren's lips purse as she continues to move. "I wanted you to come with me."

I laugh. "Aren't you thankful for my non-existent refractory period, then?"

Her eyebrows rise. "You have no idea. But does that mean if you come inside me twice that my orgasm will be twice as long as last time?"

"No. Just one time longer. Now, focus."

"I'm a woman. I can multitask. Why did you come so fast?"

It's my turn for my eyebrows to rise. What the fuck? She really wants to discuss this *while* I'm fucking her? I guess she wasn't lying about the communication thing.

"Because you're fucking hot?" It comes out as a question, because she should be completely aware of why I came so fast. But maybe the bond affects humans differently than us? I'm pretty sure she could bring me to orgasm just by talking; that's how infatuated I am with her.

"*Mmm*," she moans. "That's hot, baby. *Fuck*, can you touch me now? *Please*?"

Wrapping my tentacles around her wrists, I bring both of her hands behind her back before freeing her breasts and taking her hips in my hands.

I bring my mouth to hers, pouring all the passion I feel for her into our kiss, which easily becomes messy. We don't break apart as I hold her down so that I can pump into her with small thrusts, rubbing against her G-spot just right.

Finally, I release one of her sides and circle her clit with my thumb, ready to come with her.

"Come. For. Me. Darling," I murmur between kisses. "Milk my cock."

We erupt, my command our very undoing.

"I love you," she says, wrapping her arms around my neck as her body continues to twitch and convulse with my dick still inside of her. "I really do."

They're the most beautiful words I've ever heard in my entire life, and my heart soars with happiness I never thought I'd have the chance to experience.

Pulling Wren's face closer, I put us forehead to forehead, and we both close our eyes. "And I love you, my mate. With all I am and ever will be, I love you, and I promise to love you for the entirety of my existence, even on the most difficult days."

She kisses me softly before pulling away. "I've dreamt of you my entire life, and you know who I have to thank?"

"Who?"

"Me," she states, placing a hand to her chest. "And Freddie."

"Oh?" I ask, tilting my head to the side. "And I had absolutely nothing to do with it?"

Wren taps her chin with a finger. "Hmm. Nope. I am the one who decided to come into that spa, and Freddie here is the one that helped you find me. Looks like you had the easy job. Go figure."

I groan. "*Easy*? I had to hold you up in a pod for your entire appointment *and* give you swimming lessons."

She crosses her arms and rolls her eyes. "Oh, please. Don't act like it was torture."

I'm assuming the remnants of the extended orgasm have faded, judging by her movements. How did she become a professional at handling that so quickly?

"It wasn't," I reply, and she stills. "Because the real torture was living so many years without you. I was drowning with no rescue in sight."

Her features soften. "And now, I'm diving in with you. Figuratively speaking, anyway."

"You hear that, Freddie?" I call out behind me. "Wren is—"

But Wren cuts me off before I can finish. "I'm diving in with Alioth, Freddie!"

The fountain answers with a short burst up in the air. Seems like even he is happy our search is over.

Or maybe he's just glad I'm not so grumpy anymore.

THE END

EPILOGUE

WREN

"Are you ready for this?" I ask, staring between the dog rescue farm entrance and Alioth, nearly bursting at the seams with excitement.

He stares at the gates ahead, and his throat bobs with a big swallow. "I don't want to scare them."

"Who?"

Folding his hands in his lap, he turns his gaze to me with unsure eyes. It makes me want to crawl over this console and comfort him. "The dogs. Maybe we should actually get a pet from my planet…"

I maneuver so my whole body is facing him. "You're the one who talked me out of that because you've always wanted to know what it's like to own a dog from here. Do you want me to turn around? Because I can."

Alioth shakes his head. "No, no, no. It's okay. I just— Will you go first? I'll just stand behind, and we can go with whatever one you want."

My sweet not-so-crabby-anymore man...

Taking his hand in mine, I give it a squeeze before kissing his cheek. "I can do that, but I want you to help me make the decision, babe. It's coming home to live with *us*, not just me."

I told Alioth that a dog was the first thing I wanted, and that I'd move in the same day it came home. So, just before leaving for the farm, we finished moving the last of my things in. It is going to be so exciting, starting our little family off all at the same time.

Once we are parked and checked in, an employee leads us out to the back, where tons of dogs of all shapes and sizes frolic through what seems like quite a few acres of fenced-in land, and at least twenty more volunteers wander around and watch them.

It is a sight to behold; having the chance to see where some shelter dogs on the euthanasia list end up when the right people find them.

And we are going to have the chance to rescue one of them and take them home.

Shelby, the head volunteer, throws a thumb over their shoulder, urging us further into the acreage. We've been in constant contact for about the last month, ever since I discovered their amazing cause online. I knew from our first email that this is where we just *had* to get a dog from. Everything feels right.

"Alright. I need to get back up to the front desk, but as you can see"—Shelby swings their arms out wide—"there are tons of volunteers out here, and even more dogs. Feel free to sit, stand, wander—whatever you want, for as long as you need—until you find your perfect match."

Emotion chokes me. We are going to bring home our first baby today.

And I can't wait.

ALIOTH

Wren is quick to plant herself on her ass in the grass, which seems to send out an attention call to at least ten dogs in the vicinity.

As they near, some look up at me and hesitate, their tails slowing in wags. And for some reason, it makes me back away on instinct.

I told Wren I'd scare them, but she didn't believe me. I don't want to ruin her experience. She's been so excited about this, desperate for a dog we can introduce to our future children.

"*Every kid needs a pet*," she had told me as she broke down in tears while telling me all about her amazing childhood dog, Buddy. How wonderful it must be to experience that sort of love with a companion that can't even talk to you.

I want to know what that feels like, but I think she might have to pick the dog and help it get comfortable with me before I can do that.

Just as I turn to wander toward an empty part of land, I gasp, almost stepping on, what seems to me, a tiny creature.

With tawny fur and deep-brown eyes staring up at me, it's plopped in the perfect sitting position, with a stubby tail wagging so fast, it sends the seeds of the dandelion puff behind it soaring through the air.

Wren told me once that humans wish on pennies in fountains and dandelion puff seeds... And as silly as it sounds for a big, older, grumpy alien, I decide to try it out. What is there to lose?

I wish to bring a dog home today, whether it's this one or not. I wish for one to pick us.

I repeat the wish one more time in my mind before attempting to bend down and sit before the small beast, giving it an awkward grin.

"Hey, buddy."

The dog dashes toward me, leaping into my lap and crawling up my chest to lick at my stubble of facial hair.

Supporting its bottom so it doesn't fall, I allow it to continue its feeble kiss attack.

Laughter spills from my lips, and I don't know what it is, but something tells me to lie down and enjoy this interaction. So, I do... And before I know it, the puppy is curled up on my chest and snoring as I stare up at the pale-blue sky.

A shadow falls over us. "And you thought the dogs would be scared of you," Wren teases, staring down at me with teary eyes. "Who is this?"

"I'd like to name it Stu—"

But another volunteer cuts me off, finishing my sentence like the damn wish fairy I think she is.

"I see you've met Stub." A chill comes over me at the name I was just about to give Wren. "He was actually dumped on the street about a month ago. The vets estimate him to be about six months old."

Wren covers her mouth. "A puppy? Dumped on the street? Who could do such a thing?" She sniffs, holding a hand over her heart as she watches me hold the sleepy boy and get up to face the staff member.

The volunteer's name tag reads, *Rachel - she/her.*

"What subspecies is Stub?" I ask her.

Rachel laughs. "I'm sorry, subspecies?"

And then Wren joins in with a chuckle. "I think you mean breed, honey."

I shrug, looking to Rachel once more.

"He's a cocker spaniel, actually. He should end up weighing between twenty-five and thirty pounds."

Moving my gaze to a still-sleeping Stub, I can't help but smile at him as I pull him up to my face and breathe him in. "I really like him," I admit. "But if there's another dog you'd like…"

Wren wraps her arms around me, a soft whimper falling from her beautiful lips. "No. He's the one."

I kiss Stub's head, followed by my mate's lips, and hold a hand out to Rachel. "It was a pleasure to meet you and hear all about this little one. We'll take him."

"Shelby will take care of you inside." She brushes a finger along Stub's nose. "We'll miss you, bud. Have a wonderful life."

WREN

I cried almost the entire way home, holding on to Stub as if he might vanish at any moment, all while Alioth held on to my leg, sweeping his large thumb back and forth on my knee.

Stub's crate closes with a metal clang that thankfully doesn't wake the sleeping babe, and I wander out to find my man in the kitchen, filling up a small water dish.

"You know what I find super hot?" I ask, leaning over the kitchen island behind him.

He sets the bowl on the ground before gripping both sides of the island, staring deep into my eyes with his now-glowing orbs. "What's that?"

I whip my shirt up over my head, the only part he can see of me over the countertop covered in a lacy bra. "Dog dads."

His eyes nearly turn to ice as he assesses me with a loud gulp. "What a coincidence. I just became a dog dad today." He smirks.

"Hmm." I shrug. "Are you grumpy, too? You don't seem very grumpy, and I think crabby dog dads are pretty hot. Feels like they can boss me around in the bedroom."

The way he tilts his head at me is otherworldly, and to be honest, the more often he does it, I'm not sure if it turns me on or makes me a bit nervous. Maybe both?

In seconds, he has the island clear of his mail, before he says, "Get up on this island and crawl to me, darling."

There he is.

Using the bottom rungs of the stools for support, I climb up to the top of the counter and slowly crawl across it until I'm seated before him on the edge, my legs spread to the outside of his hips. And all the while, his transformation works its magic.

"Lie back," he orders, gently pushing me back until I'm flat.

Alioth pulls my leggings and panties off, working my legs to his liking, which end up as wide as they can go and bent, with my feet settled on the edge of the cool granite.

Then he walks away.

"Um, what are—"

But he answers by moving behind me and reaching forward to unclasp and remove my bra.

Holding his fingers above my mouth, he commands, "Suck."

I open my mouth to take his two digits in, swirling my tongue around them as they move further inside. He pulls them out, and I release them with a pop, shooting him a wicked smirk.

Within ten steps, he's back where he started, staring at my core like it holds all of life's secrets.

"Look at how pretty your swollen cunt is, dripping for me and making a mess all over my kitchen," he murmurs, using the fingers I just had in my mouth to spread my lips apart.

I can't help but squirm. "What are you going to do about it?"

He pretends to mull it over for a second before lowering himself to my mound, his facial stubble rubbing against me just right. "Eat it."

It only takes seconds for Alioth to get me on the brink of an orgasm before he pulls away.

"Hey!" I yell. "I was so close."

His mouth peppers kisses along both of my thighs, and he leans far over me. "I know, but don't you want to know how good you taste right before you finish?"

I lean up and mold my mouth to his, plunging my tongue in to taste at the same moment he sheaths himself inside me, making me gasp.

Alioth picks up the pace, pushing us both to the brink. "So, when do we get to talk about babies? Human ones."

A guffaw bursts out of me. "You want to—" I moan. "Talk about that right now?" My words are much breathier than his.

He nods, nibbling on my neck. "Yeah. Don't you humans call this practice?"

Straightening up to standing, he grabs my hips and picks up his pace. Our sweaty bodies slap together, and I can't find it in me to respond.

"*Yes*, Wren. You take me so good, baby. Come for me. Now."

His commanding tone is my undoing. I fall apart around him with a scream, raking my nails down his forearms.

Stub's screeching whines travel through the house as I ride out the waves, and Alioth goes still.

"Uh," I breathe. "Don't stop."

Alioth pulls himself free and begins furiously pumping his cock, kissing one of my knees with a grunt. His release paints my stomach, and I instantly reach out to rub it in, but his tentacles latch on to both of my wrists midair.

He growls. "You're so beautiful, painted with my cum. A true work of art."

There goes me asking about why he didn't come inside me. This man is full of so many sexy surprises.

"Now what?" I ask, batting my lashes at him.

His tentacles pull me up to sitting as his hands roam my torso and absorb his release from my skin.

After kissing my cheek, he says, "I go get Stub. He's upset." He pauses, helping me off the counter. "Or are we supposed to let him cry it out?"

ALIOTH

Barks wake Wren and me up from our spot on the floor. According to the alarm on my nightstand, it's 5:15 a.m.

"Ugh," she groans. "Shall we call it and just be up for the day?"

I answer with a huff. "Yep. We can nap when he does."

Stub rushes out from his crate, and after a potty break and breakfast, he settles between us on the couch.

"Do the swimming lessons count for Stub, too?" I ask, glancing over at my mate.

She smiles, her bedhead and cute crooked tooth warming me from the inside out. "Absolutely. I say we do all the things we want to, when we want to. What do you think?"

Leaning over Stub, I wrap my hands around her face, pulling her to me. "Yes, darling. Let's dive right into this new life. Together."

I mold my lips to hers, feeling her smile against my mouth as Stub climbs his way up our bodies and uses his nose to separate us so we can kiss him too.

ACKNOWLEDGMENTS

I'm not even sure where to begin... Especially since my Mate-Cute Series seems to have been a smashing hit! Those of you who shared the hell out of Kiran have helped me immensely in getting the word out about my alien series, and for that, I'm grateful.

The amount of people I've been blessed to know, meet, and feel supported and loved by is infinite. I know for a fact that if I were to name everyone, I'd still find a way to unintentionally miss someone, and I never EVER want to do that. So, I'll try to keep this brief and all-encompassing.

My family: I'm lucky to have the supportive family that I do. Thank you for fostering my love of reading, for pushing me to chase my dreams, and for helping me in any way, shape, or form that you can to get to where I am today. I'd be lost without all of you.

My friends: With each passing year, I am in awe of all of you. I brag about you guys to literally everyone I know, because you are once-in-a-lifetime friends. Seriously. Thank you for loving me, for supporting me, and for always being there when I need a listening ear.

You have no idea how much you all mean to me. You are seriously my chosen family.

My CPs: You are lifesavers, really and truly. It doesn't matter the timeline I'm working with, or what I've managed to forget or make a mistake on, you guys are always there to jump in and help. My books would not be what they are today without all of you. Thank you for being my CPs and my friends. I treasure you.

My sensitivity readers - *Ki Jones, Kayla H., @Readwithnyia on Instagram, and @xmanicpixiebookgirlx on Instagram*: I hope you know what you have done for me and this book is something I could never do on my own. You not only volunteered your time and energy to help me by ensuring I included the thoughtfulness, care, and respect these characters and this story deserve, but you made our discussions about everything so meaningful. Diversity, equity, inclusion, and representation in books is vital, and I owe the accuracy of those in Wren and Alioth's story to all of **YOU**. Thank you **SO** much. **XO**.

My editor, Andrea: Thank you for sharing my excitement for Wren's story, and for taking the time to work on this book. I know for a fact that I couldn't have pulled this book together, nor could I have made it what it is today, without you. So, thank you. You're truly one of the best!

My cover designer, Victoria: I already knew you would, but once again, you literally nailed this cover. I don't know how you manage to do it, but you find a way to take my jumbled mess of written explanation and inspo photos, and put it all together to create a truly perfect version of Alioth. You are one of a kind! Thank you SO much for continuing with this series with me and for creating another one of my dream covers. I'm truly appreciative.

Pen Pals: There is something so calming and safe about all of you. I always know that if I need a place to talk or vent about writing, or even just life, you will all be there for me. Again, I'm so glad we connected, because I now have even more life-long friends. **XO**.

My readers: As many of you already know, this writing journey wouldn't even be possible without you. Whether this is your first time reading something by me or not, I'm immensely grateful for you. Thank you for taking a chance on something I worked so hard on, something that's so near and dear to me, and a story I hope made you laugh. That has been the goal with this series. And for those of you who have been just as excited as I have been for Wren's story, I hope this was everything you could've hoped for. I could never thank you enough for the numerous ways you support my writing career. It means more than you could ever imagine. If you ever need a safe person, you know where to find me online.

To my dog, Finnick: You are the reason I work so hard every day, because you deserve the best life for all you do for me. I strive every day to be the human you think I am, and I never forget how lucky I am to have the goodest boy who loves me to the ends of the universe.

And finally, anyone and everyone in between: As I'm sure you can probably tell, I could make a list a mile long of people to thank for these things, and I'd still find more to thank. The list is endless, and it always will be. So, to anyone who has impacted my life, my writing, my journey in some way—thank you. I'll never stop being thankful, because I'm beyond lucky to have discovered what makes me truly happy, and I'll never stop pursuing that dream. And I'll never stop fighting for the survival of diversity, equity, and inclusion in stories, the availability of and access to books, and the art and magic of tales we all find ourselves in as a whole. **Never**.

Thank you for taking a chance on me. It means the world. I would not be here without you.

XOXO,

Meghan

AUTHOR BIO

Meghan Monarch is a romance author writing flutter-worthy love stories in various romance sub-genres. She loves athleisure wear, movie theaters, dancing in grocery store aisles, obsessing over her favorite fandoms, loud music, and even louder laughter.

She writes from her Michigan home, where she lives with her dog, Finnick—a super cool standard poodle with a colored mohawk.

When she's not writing, she's reading, working out, relaxing, or going out on solo dates and spending time with her favorite people.

Check out her website and follow her on social media using the link and QR code below to stay notified of news and updates.

www.meghanmonarch.com

ALSO BY MEGHAN

HEROES OF RED SERIES

A sequenced series that needs to be read in order

- **Book One:** *Saving Tatum* (Available NOW)

- **Book Two:** Coming in 2026!

MATE-CUTE SERIES

A collection of interconnected standalones that can be read in any order

- **Book One:** *Rooting for Kiran* (Available NOW)

- **Book Two:** *Diving in With Alioth* (Available NOW)

- **Book Three:** Coming in 2026!